"Yes, Lucas, I really would like to know."

"I often wondered what happened to you," Alina continued, full of curiosity.

"And I you, my love." Desire burned in his eyes, and with an aching groan, he gathered her close, his mouth hungrily finding hers. She had no thought to resist; of their own volition her arms crept around him.

His kiss was deep and passionate and more urgent than she had ever remembered. A moan escaped Alina as her head sank back, and his lips burned a trail down her soft neck, his hand gently caressing her breast.

But somewhere in the depths of her passion, she remembered what he had done to her. She must put a stop to this foolishness— and soon—or all would be lost....

Harlequin Romances
by Margaret Mayo

These books may be available at your local bookseller.

For a free catalog listing all titles currently available,
send your name and address to:

Harlequin Reader Service
P.O. Box 52040, Phoenix, AZ 85072-9988
Canadian address: Stratford, Ontario N5A 6W2

Return
a Stranger

Margaret Mayo

Harlequin Books

TORONTO • NEW YORK • LONDON
AMSTERDAM • PARIS • SYDNEY • HAMBURG
STOCKHOLM • ATHENS • TOKYO • MILAN

Original hardcover edition published in 1983
by Mills & Boon Limited

ISBN 0-373-02602-1

Harlequin Romance first edition February 1984

CHAPTER ONE

'You!' The colour drained from Alina's face. Her heart stopped, and if anyone had told her she had seen a ghost she would have believed them.

'Hello, Alina. It's been a long time. How are you?' Lucas Delgado's powerful frame blocked her doorway, the brown velvet eyes which she remembered so well appraised her with a slow thoroughness that set her pulses racing and left her feeling stripped and defenceless.

She gave a choking cough and her heart resumed its beating. 'Eight years, to be precise.' Initial shock changed swiftly to wild anger. 'And since you haven't bothered to contact me in all that time you can get the hell out of here now! You're not welcome.'

'Tut, tut, Alina.' Thick dark brows, which contrasted strangely with his silvery blond hair, rose in mock surprise. 'That's not ladylike. I know very well your mother brought you up better than that.'

'Maybe, but my mother's no longer alive. This is my house now and I please myself whom I invite in.' Hostile sparks flew from her eyes, which were a similar brown to Lucas's. Her hair too was only a shade darker. More than once they had been mistaken for brother and sister—except that her feelings for him had been far from sisterly!

But that was all over. The past was dead and forgotten. Her broken heart had healed—or so she had thought. As she saw him now her limbs began to shake, and rampant thoughts chased round in her mind until she was furious with herself for feeling any reaction other than stone cold hatred.

With a quick vicious movement she shouldered the door, but anticipating her rejection he stopped it with a foot clad, unexpectedly, in a brown suede Gucci shoe. He contrived to look hurt, at the same time propelling her none too gently backwards and swinging the door wide.

Eight years had changed him. At twenty-six he had been immature, tall and thin for his height, unsure of himself, easily pushed around. Now he was a broad-shouldered, virile male, and Alina could guess at the muscular strength hidden by his Savile Row suit. He carried himself with a commanding air of self-confidence, his deep tan suggesting considerable time spent abroad.

His face had developed strong lines and she quickly realised that she would be unable to twist this Lucas round her little finger. 'Suppose you tell me exactly why you're here?'

He frowned at the caustic tone in her voice. 'I never discuss business on the doorstep. Shall we make ourselves comfortable?' He strode down the hall and Alina was compelled to follow, fuming inwardly, trying unsuccessfully not to show it.

But why shouldn't she be angry? He had done the dirty on her. He had been the one to walk out without so much as one word of explanation. She ought to have had more sense than allow him into the house— except that she had not had much choice!

He settled himself into a deep armchair in what had been her mother's sitting room looking amazingly relaxed, his compelling eyes fixed on her face. He beckoned her to sit too, but she remained standing, her hands aggressively on her hips. 'You have a damn cheek! I ought to phone the police.'

'But you won't, of course,' he grinned, 'because deep down you're pleased to see me, except that you won't admit it, even to yourself.'

'The hell I am,' she snapped. He had a nerve! 'If you've turned up here hoping you can take up where you left off, you're making one big mistake.' She smoothed moist palms over her denim-clad thighs, unconsciously straightening her faded woollen sweater, wishing ridiculously that he had not caught her in her working clothes. Not that it mattered. Whatever they had had going between them was long since dead.

A frown deepened the furrows already grooved in his brow. Impatiently he ran long fingers through his thick fair hair. 'You've changed, Alina.'

'I'm twenty-four,' she returned swiftly. 'I'm no longer a schoolgirl. What did you expect?'

'At least a welcome. You make me feel a stranger.'

'Which is precisely what you are,' she snapped. 'I'm not the only one to have changed. I almost didn't recognise you. Have you come into a fortune?'

One eyebrow arched wryly. 'The outer trappings? You approve?'

'I didn't care when all you owned were patched jeans and faded shirts,' she shrugged, 'your fine clothes certainly don't impress me now.' But the man he had become impressed her, whether she liked it or not. He exuded an irresistible magnetism, certainly something far stronger that he had possessed before.

She felt it coming across in waves and had to fight not to react to it, especially when his eyes roved over her inch by inch, taking in the rounded curve of her hips, her flat stomach, the proud thrust of her breasts, finally coming to rest on her face, studying each feature in turn, so that her cheeks grew warm and she turned savagely away.

'When you've quite finished,' she said, 'I'm still

waiting to find out why you decided to look me up again.'

'I understand you've fallen upon hard times?' The brown eyes were narrowed, their expression intent and curious.

Alina tossed her head, her shoulder-length hair clinging to the faint pink bloom of her cheeks. 'And you've come to gloat? Now that you've quite clearly landed upon your feet you're going to positively relish the reversal of our roles?'

'The irony of the situation has not escaped me,' Lucas said smoothly. 'And I was sorry to hear about your parents. The accident must have been a great shock.'

'It was,' she replied tightly, 'and now you've offered your condolences you can go.'

'That's not the reason I'm here.' His glowing eyes watched her closely. 'I read your advertisement, and I've heard rumours that you're in debt up to your eyeballs. I'd like to discuss the matter.'

Alina laughed hollowly. 'Don't tell me that the poorest boy in the village is now in a position to help the girl who was once the richest? It's ludicrous!'

But even as she spoke she knew that unless the clothes he wore were borrowed, and the Lotus sports coupé standing in the drive hired, Lucas had had a drastic change of circumstances. Everything about him spelt wealth and success—and she resented it!

His mouth twisted cynically. 'Stranger things have been known to happen. Are you prepared to talk it over?'

Alina's legs trembled with the shock of Lucas appearing out of the blue, and topped with what seemed like an offer of financial help from this most unlikely source, it was more than she could take.

She groped behind for a chair and sat down without

once taking her eyes from his face. Once she had been going to marry him. Now, because of what he had done to her, she hated the very sight of him. But if he had money—and everything was kept on a strictly business level—what had she to lose? She had had no other offers.

'My parents lived beyond their means,' she admitted begrudgingly. 'I never knew. They set me up in business when I was eighteen—I have an antique shop in the village—and converted some of the rooms here into a flat, so that I could be entirely independent yet still——'

'Under your mother's jurisdiction?'

She was startled by the bitterness in his voice. 'Why do you say that?'

He laughed drily. 'We both know she ran your life. Mrs Stewart was the most possessive woman I've ever known. She had high hopes for you, did you know?'

Alina did, but loyalty forbade her to admit it. After Lucas had gone her mother had continually introduced her to the right people, hoping she would make a good match, and was absolutely distraught when her daughter showed not the slightest interest.

Mrs Stewart had despised Lucas, referring to him as 'that stable boy'. He had worked for them for ten years, during which time Alina had passed through a whole host of emotions, beginning with slavish devotion at the tender age of six, to sisterly affection, and then finally love.

'My mother loved me,' she defended strongly. 'It was only natural that she should want nothing but the best for me.'

'And for herself,' Lucas added. 'She always was on the extravagant side. I'm not really surprised that you're in trouble now.'

Alina stiffened, flinging a contemptuous glance in

his direction. 'How dare you!'

'Are you denying it? Why else are you in financial difficulties?' The cold hard light in his eyes was frightening. 'I saw it coming for years. A mere outsider I might have been, worthy only of mucking out all those expensive horses she couldn't afford to keep, but I knew what would happen.'

Alina was incensed, indignant colour burning her cheeks, her hands clutching tightly the arms of her chair. 'You have no right to talk about my mother like that!'

But he continued as though she had not spoken. 'She felt it imperative to keep up the life style to which she had been accustomed. It wasn't her fault that she came from a wealthy family, and she thought she was on to a good thing when she latched on to your father. A pity she wasn't able to see into the future. Little did she realise that a weak heart would prevent him from working, and that without him his business would go to the dogs.

But she chose to ignore that. She pushed it to the back of her mind and spent money like water, entertaining like royalty, holding on to a regiment of servants who were not really necessary. She had it coming to her. But she was more fortunate than you. She escaped before the dreadful finality caught up with her. You're the one who's left to face the consequences.'

'And you, I think, have said enough!' Alina was rigid with anger, her voice icily cold, her head tilted proudly. 'After that I wouldn't accept one penny from you!'

God, he had changed. In all the time she had known him she could never remember him making so long a speech. But it was not that. It was the insults—his derogatory remarks about her mother.

In point of fact they were true, she could not deny

it, but to have Lucas fling them at her, as though she herself were incapable of comprehending the true situation, was the last straw. Kathleen Stewart might have had her faults, but she had been her mother, and Alina had loved her.

It was her mother who had sympathised and consoled her when Lucas disappeared, her mother who had helped her through the black days. This had meant a lot to Alina. Prior to that her mother had shown distinct disapproval of their relationship, threatening to send Alina to school in Switzerland, and finally sacking Lucas.

But Alina had met him secretly. They made plans to run away and get married on her sixteenth birthday. It had all seemed so romantic.

Except that Lucas had never turned up!

For long pain-filled months she could not accept that he had walked out without a word. Each day she waited for his call, convinced he would ring and ask her to join him, trying to make herself believe that he was finding somewhere for them to live, putting her interests first.

It had been a long time before she finally admitted that it was all over. Her mother said he had gone to London; whether it was true she had no way of knowing.

Now she scarcely gave him a thought. That part of her life was over. *So what the hell was he doing here stirring it all up again?*

She leapt up and pointed a finger towards the door. 'Get out!' she shrieked.

His brows rose laconically. 'And if I don't?'

'I really will call the police.' She picked up the phone and dared him to oppose her.

Slowly Lucas pushed himself up, an amused smile playing at the corners of his sensuous lips. 'You're being melodramatic, Alina, and it doesn't suit you. What's happened to the sweet placid girl I once knew?' He moved with lithe easy grace across the room, plucking the phone easily from her nerveless fingers. 'You know very well that what I say is true, so why won't you let me help? Exactly how deeply in trouble are you?'

He was so close she could feel the warmth of his body. His six foot two towered a good eight inches above her—she had forgotten exactly how tall he was. A thread of awareness ran through her and she knew fatalistically that there was a danger of her intense anger turning into something else.

Lucas Delgado was not an easy man to hate. There was something overpowering about him, a charismatic quality that threatened to consume her.

If he had argued, retaliated with words equally as heated, she could have fought. But his whole attitude now was one of gentleness, as though he appreciated her feelings—and genuinely wanted to help!

She looked up, and as their eyes met, his dark and disturbing, her own wide and apprehensive, she felt a physical response. Her antagonism began to melt and, alarmed by the betrayal of her own body, she quickly turned. But before she could escape his fatal magnetism, he hooked a hand behind her head.

'No, Lucas, no!' She knew instinctively that he was going to kiss her and it became imperative to stop him. 'Get away and leave me alone—you've hurt me enough.'

He frowned momentarily, as though something puzzled him, then with a harsh ejaculation his mouth came down on hers, and he pulled her relentlessly against the muscle-hard strength of him.

Alina struggled futilely; pitting her strength against him was like fighting a lion. His arms were inflexible, bound round her like cords of steel. She felt the rapid beating of his heart and when she dared to look into his eyes there was a pitch of desire that confused her.

Resolutely, and with great difficulty, she stiffened, but as though goaded by her lack of emotion he increased his attack, bruising her mouth with his hard lips, demanding a response, moulding her body to him, his hands firm and insistent in their attempt to arouse.

It was though he had never been away. All fight drained out of her and, unable to help herself, Alina gave a moan of pure desire. Her lips parted to allow him to plunder the sweetness of her mouth, her arms snaked behind his neck and she gave herself in total surrender.

But a taste was all she was allowed. As suddenly as he had begun Lucas stopped. He put her roughly from him, shuttering his eyes, his face an inscrutable mask.

Alina stepped back in horror, wave upon wave of humiliation engulfing her—what had she done? What desire had possessed her? Why had she allowed herself to respond when it had been apparent that he had merely been testing her reaction?

Mortification sharpened her voice. 'Is that the way you usually do business? Is that the way you've climbed to the top?' She despised herself as much as him. 'Would bed have been the next step?'

His lips dropped, shuttering his eyes completely. 'I'm not going to apologise, but believe me, I didn't intend that to happen.'

'Good,' snapped Alina, 'because believe me, I never intended it to happen either. You mean nothing to me now.'

'If I ever did.' A glacier-like glint darkened his eyes. 'Have you any Scotch? I sure could do with a drink.'

'There may be some of my father's left,' she

shrugged carelessly. 'I don't touch it myself.' She searched a cupboard and found a quarter bottle, handing it to him silently and retreating to the far side of the room.

He poured a glass and downed it in one swallow, finishing the rest as she stood and watched, her nerves taut, feelings numbed. Never had she imagined that meeting Lucas again would be so shattering.

For years she had dreamed of such an occurrence, had hoped against hope that one day he would turn up and everything would be as it once had. But never had she realised that it would shake her so completely.

'Now what?' she asked as he placed the empty bottle on the table.

'Now I go,' he said. 'I'll come back tomorrow. Maybe then you'll have got over the shock of seeing me and be in a better position to discuss your future plans.'

Holding herself rigidly in check, Alina said tightly, 'My future plans do not include you. It would be best if you left and never came back.'

'You're in trouble,' he said. 'What are friends for if they can't help out?'

'Friends?' He had to be joking! 'You lost all claim to that eight years ago.'

His narrowed look suggested unspoken criticism. Glancing swiftly at what looked suspiciously like a Cartier watch, he strode towards the door. 'I'll see myself out. Will ten in the morning be suitable—or is that too early?'

'There's no point in you coming,' she said coldly. 'None at all.' But she knew that he would. He had developed into that type of man.

When he had gone she collapsed on to a chair, shivering uncontrollably even though the room was warm. Why had he come? *Why?* Friends are to help out, he had said, but what friend was he? She wished belatedly that she had never put the wretched advert in. But who would have expected Lucas Delgado to answer it?

He had been a poor man. His mother had brought up a large family single-handed, Lucas was the eldest and had worked at any odd job he could lay his hands on, including helping out with her parents' horses. All the money he earned had gone to his mother.

Shortly after Lucas went to London the whole family moved and no one had heard of them since. But never in her wildest dreams had Alina imagined that he would become so successful, so aggressively confident, so affluent, as he now appeared to be.

And he must have money, otherwise why would he respond to her advertisement? A partner, she had asked for, someone willing to help turn her home into flats.

Wythenhall Manor, set in the heart of the Cotswolds, was a beautiful old house built of mellow Cotswold stone, dating back to the sixteenth century, and Alina genuinely loved it. It had been a tremendous shock to discover that her parents were deeply in debt. A huge overdraft and a second mortgage amounting to tens of thousands of pounds had prompted her solicitor to advise her to sell. But Alina saw that as a last resort—hence the advertisement. It was the only way she could think to make money to pay her debts.

But for Lucas Delgado of all people to get in touch—it was entirely beyond her powers of comprehension. The shock was total. She felt devastated.

She wished with all her heart he had kept away. He had no right doing this to her. It had taken her long enough to get over him; now the old wound had opened and it was as sore as it had ever been.

Since Lucas, there had been no other man—no one

special. She had had plenty of escorts, her mother had
seen to that, but not one had matched up to him. Not
that Alina had consciously been saving herself. She
had never expected to see him again. But now she
knew without a doubt that if she couldn't marry Lucas
she wanted no one. It was that simple.

And he had made it clear he did not want her! His
kiss had been nothing more than an experiment. The
best thing she could do was make sure he did not re-
enter her life.

It was a long time before she moved and slowly
made her way up to her own flat, heating milk for a
drink which she hoped would help her sleep, but
which didn't. She lay awake for most of the night,
reliving the past, marvelling at the incredible change
in Lucas.

He was a far cry from the youth she remembered. A
hard man now, accustomed to getting his own way—
and if that meant he wanted to help her out then she
was quite sure that that was what he would do.

The pity of it was that she had had no other replies
to her advertisement. She had begun to think that
there was nothing for it but to sell. Her antique shop
did reasonably well, but certainly did not make
enough to run a house this size.

Eventually she drifted into sleep, waking several
hours later to the warmth of sunshine on her face. It
looked like being another glorious sunny day, more
like summer than spring, and she ought to feel glad to
be alive. So why didn't she?

Memories returned swiftly and she glanced at her
bedside clock. Another hour and Lucas would be here.
Sunday morning—when she usually lay in. Why
hadn't she been more firm? She didn't want him, there
was no point. He belonged to her past, not her
present.

She got out of bed and went to the window, pushing the mullioned frame wide and breathing deeply the fresh morning air. The surface of the trout lake shimmered, buds were bursting, birds fed their young in tree-top nests. Perfection! Trust Lucas to spoil it!

By the time she had washed and dressed and eaten a sketchy breakfast, Alina had worked herself into a fine state. When the doorbell rang on the stroke of ten she found it impossible to wipe the scowl from her face.

'You don't look too pleased to see me.' He had scorned his suit today for close-fitting black jeans and a thin black sweater which clung to his tightly muscled chest. The power she had only guessed at was revealed in bulging forearms, and she still couldn't get over the change in him. He had always been active, swimming in their pool when her mother was out, and a member of the local rugby team, but he had certainly had none of the muscular power he sported now.

'I'm not,' she snapped, both angry and frightened by the emotions which were chaotically churning her stomach, by her shameless response to his masculinity. 'I told you not to come. Why have you?'

'Because I don't like to see you in difficulties.'

Her over-brilliant eyes narrowed. 'You expect me to believe that? It's more likely you want to see me dragged down to the level that was once your lot in life. But I'm afraid you're wrong. No way am I going to slum it.'

His face stiffened, his handsome eyes flicked over her coldly. 'I don't like your insinuation.'

Proudly she held his gaze. 'We hardly led comparable life-styles.'

'My family have been poor,' Lucas snarled, 'but our house was spotless—and we didn't owe one cent. Nor did it seem to bother you.'

Alina's cheeks flamed and she looked away. 'It's not my fault I'm in debt now. And I can do without you rubbing salt into my wounds.'

'You loved me once,' he said, 'despite what I was, do you think I would scorn you because you've had a change of circumstances?'

'Who knows what you would do?' His attitude stung and she wanted to hit back. 'All I know is that I don't want you here now. Whether by fair means or foul you've landed on your feet, but no way are you going to lord it over me. I've had as much of you as I can stomach, and if you really do care then you'll go—because you make me sick!'

Lucas drew a swift breath and caught her shoulders, his long, lean fingers digging painfully into her soft flesh. 'You unfeeling little bitch,' he said coldly. 'I almost wish I hadn't come.'

She twisted furiously. 'Me too—and you're hurting. Let go of me!'

'I'd like to do a lot more,' he grated harshly. 'You don't deserve help.'

'I didn't ask for yours,' Alina cried, some of the fight going out of her. Lucas in this mood was frightening.

'And how many other offers have you had?' he sneered. 'Not too many people these days are prepared to part with their money, especially if they're not sure of a quick and highly profitable return.' With a savage gesture he released her, thrusting his hands deeply into his pockets and scowling ferociously.

'Then why are you here?' she demanded. 'Are you so rich you can afford to throw yours away on what you obviously consider an unviable proposition?'

He sighed impatiently. 'I came because I knew you. Because I didn't like the idea of you having to suffer.'

Ha! That was a laugh. Hadn't he made her suffer

enough eight years ago, hadn't he driven her almost out of her mind with the anguish of not knowing why he had gone or where he was? 'I'll survive,' she answered bitterly. 'Don't worry your handsome head about me.'

'I'm beginning to think I shouldn't,' he returned strongly. 'I must be a fool, but I'd still like to discuss it with you. Shall we go inside?'

Alina shrugged and turned wearily away. Trying to resist Lucas was like trying to stem a floodtide single-handed. In the sitting room of her flat he glanced appreciatively at the plain russet carpet and well-chosen pieces of furniture, different periods blending harmoniously. The curtains were moss green velvet, the colour echoed in lampshades and cushions piled on the deep settee—her only concession to anything modern.

It was ironical that once she would have given anything to be alone with him like this. Instead they had had to snatch furtive moments in the stable or tack room, away from the prying eyes of her mother.

Her mother had been amused when he had first come to work for them and Alina, a mere child of six, had followed him around like a love-starved puppy. She had adored him, even then. He was ten years older and he knew so much.

When he wasn't working or kicking a ball he had his nose stuck in a book. He had explained about the stars in the sky and the animals in the fields. She had thought he was wonderful.

It had pleased him to have her trailing after him. He had been very patient and kind, and gradually as she grew older her adoration had deepened into something else. She had experienced feelings she did not quite understand. And when one day Lucas kissed her, a brotherly kiss, nothing more, it had released a whole host of emotions, and the next time they were alone she had said innocently, 'I love you, Lucas,' quite sure that he must love her too.

There had been an expression on his face she had been unable to read, but the next second he had pulled her into his arms, his kisses then those of a man, deep and urgent, hinting at bridled passion.

When he had pulled her down on to a pile of hay and slid his hand beneath her blouse she had been shocked, but she had not resisted, and gradually there had developed a beautiful relationship between them.

She blossomed beneath his love, and her mother forbade her to see him. They met in secret and hatched their plan to run away. Emotionally, it was the most traumatic day of her life and she had felt at that time that she would never get over it.

Now Lucas was here again. They were each eight years older. A lot had happened since then and he was, if anything, even more disturbing.

When she was fifteen and innocent and in love for the first time he had been her hero. Now, tanned, muscled and exuding a wild primitive magnetism, he made her pulses race faster than ever. Although she wanted desperately to hate him, although he angered her intensely, deep down Alina knew that nothing had changed. All these years her love had lain dormant. One kiss had brought it surging to life, it was going to be the most difficult thing she had ever done to keep it under control.

He sat down. 'Do you mind if I smoke?'

She said tightly, 'Would it matter if I did?'

He glanced at her darkly and there was silence for a few moments as he lit his cigar. The padded Louis XV chair made him look ridiculously uncomfortable.

'I've been thinking,' he said, 'about this place. It would make an ideal conference centre.'

'Would it?' queried Alina coldly. 'But I don't want a conference centre. I want to turn it into flats—beautiful, elegant flats, flats for the rich.'

He ignored her. 'Your father showed me two huge rooms. They'd be ideal for meetings, seminars, film shows, etc. And you have sufficient bedrooms to put up the delegates, most with adjoining bathrooms, I believe?

'And, of course, there's your trout lake, the swimming pool, horse riding, plenty of sport or relaxation for when the meetings are over. And the cost to get it ready would be negligible compared with your idea.'

'And you think business men would travel out here for their conventions, or whatever?' she asked scathingly. 'Isn't it asking rather a lot?'

'Properly organised and successfully advertised it could make a huge profit. Situations like this are popular, didn't you know? A little relaxation away from the rat-race.'

Alina sat down on the settee, stretching out her legs and crossing her slim ankles. She tucked her hands behind her head and looked at him with what she hoped was the right amount of uninterest, even though something told her that he had hit upon a brilliant idea.

'I've told you, it's out of the question.'

Every fibre of her being was aware of him. He had matured into the type of man any woman would give her eye teeth for, and she wondered whether this confident, arrogant—yes, definitely arrogant, person really was the same one she had spent so much time with all those years ago.

Gone was the flippancy, the couldn't-care-less attitude, the bounce of youth. Instead a shrewd business brain ticked inside his head and he assessed every situation carefully. Even now he watched her closely, reading her thoughts, knowing exactly what he was going to say and when he was going to say it.

She wanted to ask all sorts of questions. She wanted to know why he had left without a word, where he had been, what he had been doing, how he had earned his money. But she knew that now was not the moment. Indeed, she might never discover the answer.

Whereas once she could have asked him anything she knew that at this moment it would be like questioning a total stranger. That was what he had become. This big man who sat opposite her, completely relaxed, perfectly at home, he wasn't the Lucas she had once known and loved.

'You're a fool,' he said, a hard light in his eyes. 'This could be the making of you. Doesn't the idea of such a centre appeal? You wouldn't spoil the character of the house—and you could still keep on this flat for your personal use.'

'You have it all worked out.' She sounded bitter.

'I thought you'd be relieved. You looked like one worried woman the last time I was here.'

I was worried, I still am worried, she thought—but it was not nice to be told it was so obvious. She shook her head angrily. 'I don't think there's anything further to discuss.'

Impatiently his fingers strummed on the arm of the chair. 'What alternative have you?' His angular face looked bitter as though he was wondering how on earth she could afford to turn down his offer. 'None,' he snapped, without waiting for her answer. 'Except to sell. I've been checking. The sort of money you owe you'll never get out of debt, and converting into flats will be a dead loss. You'll never recoup the cost of that, not for years, and somehow I don't think your creditors will wait that long.'

Alina shot up from her seat. 'You have a damn cheek! It has nothing to do with you what I owe. How dare you!' She stamped her foot angrily. '*How dare you!*'

Lucas stubbed out his cigar and stood up to face her, smiling calmly, tolerantly. 'If things had gone according to plan it would have been very much my business.'

'But since they didn't,' she yelled angrily, 'you had no right. Why didn't you stay out of my life? I don't need you!'

His eyes penetrated her face. 'But you need someone. Why shouldn't it be me? You know the old saying, better the devil you know——'

'That's the trouble,' she scoffed. 'I know you too well.' She wished he wouldn't look at her like that, it made it very difficult to stand up to him. 'My idea of a partner was a perfect stranger, someone with whom I could have a business relationship, nothing more.'

'And you think I'm after something else?'

'I don't know what you're after,' she snapped, 'all I know is that it wouldn't work. I don't want you anywhere within a hundred miles of me.'

Lucas seemed to stop breathing and his face became enigmatic, all feelings shuttered. 'You hate me that much?'

She lifted her slim shoulders. 'You could say that.' Perhaps it might be better this way.

'I see.' He turned away, and she had the strangest feeling that he was hurt, which was ridiculous when one thought about it. Why should it worry him? He had not bothered once in eight years to contact her. He had made it clear she no longer meant anything to him—if indeed she ever had. He could have been playing around. She had been far too young and inexperienced to know any difference, all she had known was that she loved him deeply—and always would!

'In that case, as you say, there's no point. I'm sorry to have taken up your time.' He looked directly at her again, the velvet brown eyes reproachful. 'Goodbye, Alina.'

He strode towards the door and Alina checked a sob. Now was no time to get emotional. This was by far the best solution.

At the door Lucas turned and plucked a card from his pocket. 'You can get in touch with me here if you change your mind—or if things get really desperate.' He slung it on a table near the door.

'You're still willing to help?' The whispered words were out before she could stop them.

He nodded. 'Call me a fool, if you like, but that's the way I am.'

But Alina knew she would not contact him. She was not strong enough to suffer the pain of loving a man who had nothing but an impersonal interest in her.

CHAPTER TWO

PICKING up Lucas's card, Alina slung it into the fireplace. Why, oh, why hadn't he kept away? Now her heartache had started all over again.

She could feel his presence, the lingering odour of cigar smoke filled her nostrils. She sat in the chair he had used and it was almost as though he was embracing her. She closed her eyes, listening to the sound of her own quickened heartbeats, and decided she was a fool for sending out of her life the only man she had ever loved. Her body ached for the fulfilment that he alone could give.

Why had she done it? Wouldn't a business relationship have been better than nothing at all? But the answer was always the same. It would end in disaster. Lucas wouldn't get hurt, he was far too tough for that these days, but she would. She would finish by being a wreck of a woman—was that what she wanted for herself?

She too had become independent; Lucas wasn't the only one to have changed. She had her shop, and this beautiful home—which she intended fighting to keep.

In some ways, she supposed she was like her mother. She liked it here. She liked the feel of the place, the spacious rooms, the life style. Not that she was a snob, at least she did not think so. After all, she had been prepared to marry Lucas—and he had had nothing.

If it was within her power to stay she was going to. There must be someone other than Lucas willing to invest.

But over the next few weeks, even though she advertised constantly, she had no luck, and her solicitor continued to press her to sell. 'It's all you can do,' he said. 'You'll never raise enough money otherwise. Even your idea of turning Wythenhall Manor into flats won't solve your immediate problems.'

Which was precisely what Lucas had said, damn him!

And, as though she hadn't enough troubles with the house, her shop sales began to fall. Why, she hadn't a clue, but they did, and it worried her. It also gave her more time to think about Lucas—he was as much in her thoughts these days as he had been when he first left, and she knew that her disturbed nights were beginning to tell on her appearance.

An important sale was looming up, one which Alina would normally have attended, with a good idea by now what it was she intended bidding for. This time she had not even bothered to obtain a catalogue. She wondered whether it was worth going, the way business was. What was the point in buying if she was not going to be able to sell?

But in the end she went. She had to make a determined effort. Perhaps new stock would boost sales—and she simply could not afford to let the business go. If this failed she really would be in trouble.

In a modest sort of way Alina had made a name for herself, and there were many people she knew attending the sale. Talking to them helped take her mind off her personal problems, made her realise that she ought to get out and about more, instead of brooding over her troubles. Instead of brooding about Lucas!

It looked like being a long day. It was a big sale and

there were more lots than usual, some of the ones Alina was interested in not coming up until towards the end.

It also turned out to be a frustrating day, because no matter how high she went some bidder on the other side of the room increased it. She could just see the flick of a catalogue and felt a sense of doom as the Georgian writing table she had set her mind on went the same way as the Victorian gold chaise-longue and the Minton china toilet set.

By evening all she had bought was a few items of silver, and she felt both tired and dispirited, and not a little angry at the unknown bidder. It was as though he had been doing his best to put a stop to her buying, because she had noticed that he had not bothered with any of the lots she had not been interested in herself.

She smiled ruefully at Dave Felton, a man who kept a shop in the next town. 'Not my day,' she confessed. 'I almost wish I hadn't come. Who was that bidding against me? Anyone you know?'

Dave shook his head. 'Though I did hear a whisper that there's a new chain of shops being opened throughout the Cotswolds. Some big concern intent on ousting us small traders out of business, I've no doubt. He could be buying for them.'

'But why bid against me and no one else?' cried Alina. 'That's what I don't understand. He didn't bother with you or John, or any of the others. Do you think it's because I'm a woman?'

Dave grinned. 'It stands a chance. Some folks get a kick out of that sort of thing. Never mind, there's another sale next week at Stow. Perhaps you'll do better then.'

Alina doubted it. She doubted whether she would even bother going. But deep down she knew she must, her livelihood depended on it.

But the same happened again, a different man, but even so, only outbidding her, no one else. She was furious, but no matter how many enquiries she made no one seemed to know anything about him.

It was purely by chance that she overheard her name mentioned in the café one lunch time. She had gone in for her usual sandwich and cup of tea and finding her normal table occupied had sat in a corner where she was partially hidden from the rest of the room.

'I feel sorry for Alina.' The voice belonged to Mrs Smith, a woman who had infrequently over the last years bought a few bits and pieces from her.

'But even so, there's no need for that.' Her companion was unknown. 'She ought to be reported, passing things off as genuine when they're nothing but reproduction. I know she's had a bit of bad luck and she needs the money, but that's downright criminal.'

'And the prices in that new shop in Cheltenham are way below hers, that's what I can't understand,' added Mrs Smith. 'I always thought she was very fair, but it's made me think. I mean, I have spent quite a bit of money with her. Not that I shall go again, she's lost my business.'

'And everyone else's, I shouldn't wonder,' said the unknown person bitterly.

Enraged colour flooded Alina's cheeks, but as she was about to make her presence known the two women got up and left. Perhaps as well. It could have been embarrassing tackling them in front of the other customers.

But she was determined to find out who had been slandering her name, and had a feeling that this shop in Cheltenham could have something to do with it—that and the unknown bidders at the sales.

She went back to her shop and pinned a notice on

the door saying that she would be closed for the rest of the day, then she drove her mini as fast as she dared into nearby Cheltenham.

She found the place she was after in the Promenade, a wide spacious street, lined with trees and statues, and housing the better class shops. She knew it the moment she saw it, because it had certainly not been there the last time she visited this town.

The showrooms were magnificent, taking over two floors, and she was amazed at how competitive the prices were. She was no idiot when it came to antiques and knew full well that they could command better prices—so what were they playing at? Like Dave Felton had said, they must be trying to put all the small shops out of business, then once they had the monopoly, their prices would inevitably go up.

She spent a good hour browsing, noticing that the shop was attracting a great deal of attention and business was good. At length a well dressed, city-type gentleman came up to her. 'Can I help you?'

Alina flashed her brown eyes. 'Yes, you can. 'Her voice was high, quite unlike her normal well-modulated tones. 'Does this shop belong to you?'

He looked surprised. 'No, it doesn't, I'm the manager here. But if there's anything you particularly want to know I'm sure I can help.'

Alina tilted her chin and eyed him coldly. 'I want to know who owns this shop.'

'You have a complaint?' Again a surprised lift of his brows.

'Not against you personally,' she snapped, 'unless you're the one who's going around telling everyone that my prices are too high and my stuff not genuine.'

He looked suddenly wary. 'Should I know you?'

She paused a moment and then said slowly, 'I'm Alina Stewart. I own Alina's Antiques in Wythenhall.

Does that mean anything to you?' She drew herself up and looked him directly in the eye.

Unable to hold her gaze, he busied himself lighting a cigarette. 'When I got this job I was told to make sure I told my customers that ours were the lowest prices in the Cotswolds. But I haven't mentioned any names. In fact I don't know any—I'm a stranger to this part of the country.'

His London accent confirmed that, but Alina was not so sure that she believed him entirely. 'And who told you to say that?'

'Mr Delgado, miss. This is only the first of many shops that he's opening. He should do well. He knows a lot about antiques and he certainly has a good head for business—I say, are you all right?'

Alina had gone pale and held on to an ebony armoire for support. Whatever she had thought she had never suspected that Lucas was behind all this. It was quite beyond her powers of comprehension. 'Lucas Delgado?' she managed to whisper.

He nodded and led her to a chair. He looked worried. 'Would you like a glass of water?'

She shook her head, the initial shock receding. 'I feel better now—I—I had no lunch—I suppose that's it.'

The manager looked relieved. 'Would you like a biscuit—or a sandwich? I can send for some.'

'Nothing,' she said, pushing herself up. 'I—I'll go now—I've found out what I wanted.'

He accompanied her to the door. 'Do you know Mr Delgado, Miss Stewart?'

She smiled wanly. 'A long time ago—a very long time.'

As soon as she reached home she retrieved Lucas's card from the fireplace. It had slid behind the ornamental basket of logs and got forgotten.

The Delgado Group. Very impressive! And an address and telephone number in London. Alina dialled impatiently, angry words on the tip of her tongue, only to discover to her frustration that he was out.

His secretary said she would ask him to ring her, but she wanted to speak to him now, while she was still fuming over her discovery.

He wanted to ruin her, that much was clear. And it looked as though his reason for coming here in the first place had been to spy out the way things were, not because he had wanted to help.

The more she thought about this the more angry and resentful she became, and the more humiliated when she recalled how she had responded to his kiss. That must have amused him, even though he didn't show it at the time.

For the rest of the day Alina waited in vain for his call. In fact it was two days before she heard anything, and then it was simply a message from his secretary to say that he would be calling to see her the next day.

'But I don't want to see him,' argued Alina. 'What I have to say can be said over the telephone. Why didn't he ring me like I asked?' Damn the man! Did he think she had changed her mind, or something? Was that why he was coming?

'Mr Delgado is a very busy man,' said the smooth, clear voice. 'I only saw him for a few minutes this morning. I passed on your message and he asked me to phone you.'

'Then give me his home number,' Alina snapped edgily. 'I don't want him here.'

'I'm sorry, I'm not allowed to give anyone his private number.'

'But I'm an old friend.' Alina was growing more and

more irate with each passing second. 'He won't mind me having it.'

'I'm sorry,' returned his secretary politely. 'I have my orders and——'

Alina slammed down the phone. Damn Lucas! Damn his loyal secretary!

But later, when her initial anger had subsided, she decided it might not be a bad thing. She had plenty to say to Mr Lucas Delgado, things that were perhaps not fit to be heard over the telephone.

She slept little and the next morning drank numerous cups of black coffee, unable to face the thought of food. She had no idea when he would arrive, but rather than go to the shop and have him chasing after her, she rang a friend who helped occasionally and arranged for her to take over for the day.

Jittery with nerves when midday arrived and he had still not put in an appearance, she took off the pretty blue dress she had donned earlier. The colour suited her and she knew she looked her best in it, and it had boosted her confidence which was what she needed right now—but she was not out to impress, a flaming row was on the books.

Consequently when she opened the door to him two hours later Alina wore a neat grey flannel skirt topped with a crisp white blouse which fastened demurely at the neck. She had wound her long ash-blonde hair into a coil on the top of her head and kept her make-up to a mere hint of eyeshadow and a shimmer of lip gloss.

The flicker of a smile touched her lips as their eyes met. 'Do come in.'

Another Savile Row suit sat perfectly on his broad, powerful shoulders, trousers hugging lean hips and muscular thighs. There was not an ounce of superfluous flesh on him and he looked very much what he was—a successful tycoon.

Also an unscrupulous one, she reminded herself sharply, as a familiar response to his virility tore through her.

He eyed her trim uniform with some amusement. 'Dressed for business, I see? You look as though you've spent some sleepless nights, though. I hope they were not on my account?'

'You swine!' she hissed, uncaring that he was baiting her and that she had fallen into his trap. 'It has everything to do with you, as you well know, and I have a lot I want to say to you, but not here.'

She led the way into a high, timbered-ceilinged room, with a flagged stone floor and dark panelled walls. An immense table was surrounded by chairs and her mother had used it for her popular dinner parties. At the other end easy chairs circled an open stone fireplace, logs already piled in readiness.

Although it was vast the room had character and was in no way unwelcoming. Lucas looked about him, nodding in a satisfied sort of way.

Alina perched on the edge of a chair, trembling so much it was impossible to stand, dismayed when he took the seat next to her, sitting so close that his thigh almost rubbed her own. It was impossible to contain the raw emotion his presence caused and it puzzled her how she could react like this.

At one time she had thought her feelings dead. After her initial heartbreak she had hated him passionately, had sworn that if he ever turned up she would tell him exactly what she thought of him.

Now she was trembling like a jelly, longing for the feel of his mouth against hers, her breasts aching for his touch. She shook her head, trying to dispel these irrational feelings, but before she could speak Lucas placed a set of documents on the table in front of her.

Frowning, Alina tried to concentrate, but the letters danced before her eyes and she had to make a determined effort before she realised what it was. She ought not to have been surprised.

Her face flamed and she threw it back at him. 'You know what you can do with that!'

He frowned. 'Isn't that why you wanted to see me? I thought you'd had a change of heart. It is a woman's prerogative.' He looked calm and unruffled and she could have hit him. He was deliberately aggravating her.

'Why are you trying to put me out of business?' she demanded abruptly.

'Am I?' Cool brown eyes looked into hers.

'You know very well you are.' Furiously she banged her hands on the table. 'Do you deny opening an antique shop in Cheltenham?'

A dark brow quirked in amusement. 'So? It's a free country, and as I've learned a lot about antiques over the past years it seemed a good idea to——'

'Open in opposition to me,' she accused harshly. 'The next thing you'll be having one here.'

'Oh, no.' He shook his head. 'The village wouldn't take two. Besides, Cheltenham's much bigger and busier, it has to do better. I'm surprised you didn't open your shop there.'

'It might be bigger, but there's also more competition,' she said tightly. 'No, thank you, I'm very happy where I am. Or at least I was, until you began making things difficult for me. Exactly what is your idea? There is such a thing as slander. I'd be perfectly within my rights going to the police.'

She shifted uncomfortably. It was not easy trying to argue when his very presence set her on fire, when her whole body was shamelessly crying out for his touch.

But his face tightened, a brief puzzled frown creasing his brow. 'Slander? If I were you I'd get my facts right before making such accusations.'

'So it wasn't you who put the tale about that I'm selling reproductions as the genuine article? I have another enemy, do I?' Alina's eyes flashed scornfully. 'Do me a favour, Lucas, admit that you're out to break me, that your whole story about wanting to help is a load of bull, that what you really want is for me to be out on the street without a penny to my name.'

He looked at her coldly. 'That hardly comes into it. Even if you were forced to sell there'd be sufficient funds to buy a smaller house and give you a comfortable living. Have you no idea how much this place is worth?'

His casual attitude angered her even further. 'I suppose you're an expert on property as well?'

'I know a fair bit,' he admitted, 'and if you're really dead set against me becoming your—er—partner, and you do plan to sell, I'd be interested.'

'You?' Alina could not contain her amazement. 'You have that sort of money?' She knew full well the market value of Wythenhall Manor and its estate, and it was no small sum.

'I could raise it.' A cool smile hovered.

'A real rags to riches tale,' she scoffed.

Lucas looked angry. 'If a person is determined enough to succeed, I see no reason why he shouldn't— and I certainly had sufficient incentive.'

She let that slide over her. 'I'm happy for you,' she said primly.

'Are you?' His thickly fringed eyes were bitterly sceptical. 'Then you have a funny way of showing it. But I didn't come here to argue, so far as I'm concerned we have a business deal to discuss.'

'Like hell we have!' snapped Alina, picking up the

contract and tearing it cross the middle. 'You know what you can do with that.' Belligerently she looked at him, annoyed to see him smiling. But as she looked into his eyes the familiar weakness assailed her and angrily she turned away. 'Why, Lucas, why are you doing this?' What had she ever done to make him loathe her?

He stood up and walked over to one of the small Gothic windows. Outside a splendid display of daffodils danced in the breeze, rooks cawed in the treetops, the sky was a heavenly blue. It should have been a perfect day.

For a few minutes he was silent, then he turned, pushing his hands deeply into his trouser pockets. 'Whatever you may think, Alina, I've not said one word against you or your shop.'

Silhouetted against the clear bright day, his silvery hair stood out like a halo. He looked like some blond god looking down on her from his great height. His power was supreme, his word law.

'You expect me to believe that?' Her eyes were wide and challenging. 'What sort of a fool do you take me for? It's far too much of a coincidence. Oh, no, you can deny it all you like, but I won't believe you, not ever.'

His eyes darkened ominously and he looked as though he could cheerfully have hit her, his fists clenching and unclenching at his side. 'You believe what you like, Alina. My conscience is clear.'

He spoke softly, menacingly, and she shivered, glad he was capable of controlling himself. She did not fancy being on the receiving end of those massive fists. But she was not going to give in without a fight. 'I have only your word,' she tossed savagely. 'Give me proof and I might believe you.'

'Hell!' He picked up a chair and straddled it. 'Were you always this bloody impossible?'

'Not that I remember,' she replied sweetly. 'But when something like this happens, when my livelihood is threatened, it makes me fighting mad.'

'And I'm the scapegoat?'

Across the table she could see the deep lines scored on the planes of his face, his lips were harder, firmer, but still sensual. The arrogant nose that she had used to tease him about suited him now. 'You're the cause,' she said bitterly. 'I should have known you wouldn't admit it.'

Lucas sighed wearily. 'I can see us getting nowhere with this argument. I suggest you shut up and forget it. Suppose you tell me what you're going to do about this place? You do want to stay? It would break your heart to sell?'

She nodded, lips compressed, brown eyes hostile.

'Then read through my offer. I'm sure you'll find it very fair.' He took another copy from his inside pocket, smiling grimly. 'I anticipated you well.'

Alina shrugged. What had she got to lose? A few minutes of her time? A few minutes' more agony being in the same room?

Aware that he watched she read the first page. Lucas intended footing the bill for any work that needed doing, any expenses incurred in getting the guest rooms ready, supplying any equipment. He would install whatever staff were necessary and Alina could still keep on her flat.

She turned the page. It did seem fair. Perhaps she could do worse than accept his offer? She looked across and gave him a weak smile.

'Read on,' he encouraged.

But it was an effort to tear her eyes away from his face. An invisible magnetic force drew her to him, and she would have liked to just sit and study this new and enigmatic Lucas.

Somehow she managed to drag her attention back to the closely typed pages. Lucas had full control until such time as profits equalled one half of the market value of Wythenhall Manor, after he had taken out his initial expenses and the settlement of her debts. Until then Alina kept her own flat in order—and paid the cost of running it! In fact paying him a rent for living there!

The colour drained from her face. He had a nerve! Did he really think she would agree to this? She read on, wondering what other delights he had in store for her.

She would have nothing at all to do with the running of her home as a conference centre; Lucas would deal with that. Once they were on an equal footing she would qualify for a half share of the profits.

When she had read right to the last dot she raised her eyes to his. 'If you think I'm going to sign this——' her voice was cool and almost controlled, 'you're mistaken.'

'I've given it a great deal of thought,' he said, smiling thinly. 'I think you'd be getting away lightly. I presume you can afford to keep yourself?'

'Don't be insulting,' she snapped. 'But why should you reap all the benefits? Why should I be penalised? What you're saying is that I shall be a prisoner in my own home, confined to my quarters. It's a self-contained flat, use it as such, full stop. Thank you very much, Lucas—you're just the type of friend I need!'

His eyes narrowed and hardened. 'Get off your high horse, Alina. You can't afford to turn me down.'

'But your terms are ludicrous,' she argued vehemently. 'There's only going to be one winner, and that's you.'

'Not in the long run.'

'And how long will I have to wait before any profits come my way?'

'And how long could you have struggled to make ends meet if I hadn't happened along?'

'I'd have managed, something would have turned up.' Wishful thinking, she knew, but she had no intention of admitting failure to him.

He stood up again angrily. 'God, Alina, you make me sick! How the hell could you have managed? The way you're going you'll have the house sold from under you and come out with nothing. Have some sense, woman!'

Alina gritted her teeth, refusing for several long seconds to look at him. What really galled was the idea of him being virtual owner of this house. A stable-hand, that was all he had been! A scruffy lad from the village.

And now—he dared to stand here and lord it over her! And this was only a beginning. Who knew what he would be like once he firmly had his foot in the door? She shook her head. It was impossible; she simply couldn't agree. This was *her* house. *She* owned it. If anyone had a say in the running of it, it should be her—not this detestable man who, because he had somehow accumulated a considerable fortune, thought it spoke for him.

'I can't do it.' She looked at him then, her eyes wide, her face pale.

Lucas drew a deep breath and muttered something she did not quite catch. 'You're a damned fool, a damned stubborn fool. This is by far the best offer you're likely to get. But I'm certainly not begging you to take me up on it. I shall be staying at the Coach House until the end of the week. If you change your mind get in touch with me there.'

She let him go; there did not seem much else to say. He had put her in an impossible situation. She felt as if she had been kicked on the backside. Didn't he realise exactly how much this place meant to her? Why relegate her to her own quarters? Why make sure she had nothing to do or say in the running of it? This was what hurt. She had wanted a partner, she had wanted a say in everything that went on.

He was being unnecessarily cruel. A financial injection, the place needed, that was all. She hadn't asked for a take-over bid. But he had driven her into a corner whether she liked it or not. Him and his damn shop—or shops? Who knew how many he had opened? He was slowly putting on the pressure until finally he knew she must succumb.

CHAPTER THREE

In the days that followed Alina knew that she had no choice but to take up Lucas's offer. Trade was completely dead. Not one single customer, or even prospective customer, had passed over her doorstep in a whole week. Lucas's campaign was working far better than he could have hoped.

Sooner or later she would have to contact him. Even agreeing to his ludicrous terms would be better than selling out completely and having Lucas install himself in her place. That she could never accept.

About to close the shop one evening, she was in her little back room gathering up her bag and coat when the doorbell jangled.

This was such an unusual occurrence these days that she was out like a shot, but her welcoming smile faded when she saw Lucas's bulk dominating the doorway. 'Oh, it's you. I thought you'd gone back to London.'

'Without saying goodbye? I couldn't do that.' He glanced casually about her tiny shop. 'You have this set out nicely. How's trade?'

There was no mistaking the light in his eyes. 'I think you know,' she returned coldly. 'No way can I compete with you. My entire stock would fit into one corner of your premises. I don't know why I bother.' She did not realise how bitter and disillusioned she sounded.

'Then why not join forces? It's by far the best solution.'

'The way things are going,' she said tiredly, 'I won't even be able to afford the rent on my flat.'

'You think I'd kick you out?' Lucas watched her closely.

She tossed her head. 'I wouldn't put anything past you. You're certainly not the man I once knew, or thought I knew.'

'And judging by your tone it's not a change for the better. You disappoint me.'

'*I* disappoint *you*?' Had he any idea what he was doing to her? They moved outside and he stood patiently while Alina locked the door, then tucked his hand beneath her elbow and led her to his waiting car.

And she let him! It was not until he had opened the door that she remembered her little Mini parked round the back of the shop. 'What am I doing?' she asked. Or more accurately, what was this man doing to her? He was making her lose her senses. 'You're confusing me, Lucas. I have my own car.'

'Which you won't need if you're dining out with me. You can pick it up later.'

She looked at him swiftly. 'I'm not. I'm going home.'

He grinned. 'You have no choice. When I make up my mind I usually get what I want.'

This she could well believe, and she sat back reluctantly in the low-slung coupé which smelled of leather. She was learning that to argue with Lucas got her nowhere.

As he started the engine and moved away she decided he handled his cars like he did women, manipulating them with quiet confidence, knowing how to get out of them exactly what he wanted.

How many women had he had in these eight years? she wondered, and it hurt, the thought of Lucas with someone else. But it was obvious a man as virile as he would not lead a life of celibacy.

Even now, sitting beside him, hating him, she was not totally immune. It was impossible to ignore his long lean length, and her eyes were constantly drawn to the firm brown hand on the gear knob, so close to her leg. She felt awareness tingle through her and wished she had been strong enough to refuse him.

'Where are we going?' she asked, and her voice sounded strange, strangled almost, slightly afraid.

He looked across and laughed. 'A drive—it's too early yet to eat. London is all right, but nothing can compete with the Cotswolds in springtime. I didn't realise exactly how much I'd missed it.'

She glanced at him sharply. This did not match his new image. She wondered whether he was making fun of her. But he looked perfectly serious, so she sat back and said nothing, deciding she might as well make the best of an unfortunate situation.

After a while it occurred to her that it was quite pleasant sitting beside Lucas, so long as she ignored the erratic beating of her heart. He drove carefully and not too fast and she had time to look about her, to view the peaceful farms in little dips, catch glimpses of the River Windrush as the road followed its curves. Daffodils grew in abundance, so too did primroses and purple fritillaries.

Lucas stopped the car and they listened to blackbirds and thrushes, and the plaintive sound of the willow wren. They walked across a stone-slab bridge and climbed a hill. They rested against a stone wall and it was as though the clock had been put back.

Almost without thinking she touched his arm. 'Do you remember when——' She stopped abruptly. The past had no place in their lives. That was over, finished long ago. The Lucas Delgado who had worked for her parents was an entirely different person from the Lucas Delgado who stood at her side now.

He looked at her expectantly when she did not finish.

'It doesn't matter,' she said, and disappointingly he did not press her, as she had half expected he might. It proved that he had no interest in the past. All that mattered to him was the acquisition of Wythenhall Manor, another way of making money—and at her expense! It made her feel very bitter.

The meal was excellent, but conversation was difficult. Whatever they had had in common eight years ago was non-existent, at least on Lucas's side. Alina preferred to ignore her own feelings—they were too disturbing by far. She was a business acquaintance—nothing more, and he talked about his plans as though it was a foregone conclusion that she would ultimately sign the contract.

Alina let him get on with it. She was in no rush to let him know she had made up her mind—and besides, she wanted her solicitor to vet the contract first. Lucas was devious and cunning—she had to make sure that the contract was as she understood it, that he was not doing her out of everything altogether.

However, despite all this she could not help but admire him. She had never imagined when he worked for them that he would one day develop into a successful businessman. She would have liked to ask how it happened, but he was unapproachable. The easy relationship they had once enjoyed, when they could discuss anything and everything under the sun, had gone.

She could not help feeling, though, that somewhere beneath the surface veneer of toughness still remained a fragment of the old Lucas. On one or two occasions she had surprised him looking at her with a peculiar expression that had reminded her of him as he once was. It disappeared the instant she looked at him, replaced by a mask of indifference—and it puzzled her.

It also hurt. He had gone away, had left her to her tears and heartache, had not sent so much as one word of explanation. And now he treated her as a complete stranger—as though there never had been anything between them.

There was only one thing to do, and that was treat him in a like manner. But how could she react indifferently to a man she loved? Sitting next to him in the intimate atmosphere of the Coach House's small dining room was sufficient to accelerate her pulses alarmingly and render the succulent pheasant almost tasteless.

She tried keeping her attention on her plate, but time and time again her eyes were irresistibly drawn to him, and her heart lurched painfully. It was no good trying to kid herself that he meant nothing to her, that they could enjoy a successful relationship without becoming personally involved. It simply wouldn't work.

After their coffee he sat back and lit a cigar, his steady gaze fixed on her face. 'You're still as beautiful as ever, Alina. I'm surprised you're not married.' His eyes dropped, appraising her slowly, dwelling on the proud thrust of her breasts through the cream silk shirt.

She felt her body respond shamelessly and grew angry with herself. 'I almost was,' she exclaimed bitterly, unthinkingly. 'Now my shop takes up most of my time.'

'Not so much that you can't lead a social life, surely?'

Alina's shoulders lifted in an indifferent shrug. 'Maybe I don't want to.'

'Still waiting for Mr Right to come along?' His voice was deeply cynical. 'Mind you don't leave it too long.'

She glared hostilely. 'Are you suggesting that I'm in danger of being left on the shelf?'

He smiled, more to himself than to her. 'Somehow I don't think that will happen.'

And if it does it will be your fault, she decided crossly. He had absolutely no feelings; somewhere on his way to the top he had lost them. He had become an insensitive character with no thought for anyone else. What a question to ask! Surely he must have realised the effect it would have on her? She wondered whether he had married, whether this accounted for his indifference.

Without stopping to think she put the question. 'Have you a wife, Lucas?'

'Would it matter if I had?' A mobile brow lifted.

Alina grew warm. He must know the answer to that. She had loved him to distraction and kept none of her feelings hidden. At all times she had been totally honest, with the innocence of youth declaring her love frequently, confident that he felt the same way. And eight years' absence did not change a thing like that. He had been the only man for her then, and he was the only one now—despite his harsh treatment.

But she had her pride—and tossed her head scornfully. 'I really couldn't care less, but if you have I shouldn't think she'd take kindly to you inviting other girls out to dinner.'

'Would you object, if you were my wife?' His dark velvet eyes were unfathomable, but there was a stillness about him as though somehow the answer was important.

He was certainly adept at kicking below the belt! Alina tensed, her facial muscles rigid. 'I imagine I would.' She surprised herself by sounding cool and indifferent.

And yet the answer did not seem to satisfy him. He withdrew into himself, slipping on again the mask to which she was becoming accustomed but could not understand.

'I think it's time I went,' she said, and judging by the way he immediately jumped up the evening had clearly been as much of a strain for him as it had for herself.

Lucas drove back to the shop and waited while she started up her Mini. She wound down her window and said demurely, 'Thank you for a pleasant evening, Lucas. Goodnight.'

'I'll follow you home,' he said brusquely.

'Why?' she demanded. Hadn't he seen enough of her?

'One never knows who might be lurking around. In fact I'm not sure that I like the idea of you living alone. There's no one to hear if you're in trouble, no one to call.'

He really did look concerned, which was ridiculous. All these years he hadn't given a damn whether she was alive or dead. Why the sudden interest now?

She laughed lightly. 'This isn't London—things like that don't happen here. Save your petrol, Lucas, I'll be fine.'

She shot off into the darkness, but a glance in her interior mirror showed that he had followed, and she grimaced wryly. Goodness knows what he was trying to prove. Perhaps he felt guilty? Perhaps he felt responsible now that her parents were dead? He needn't bother; she could manage very well without him.

After garaging the car she was disconcerted to find that he was still there. She turned her key in the lock, opened the door, then said, 'There, are you satisfied now?'

Light spilled out on to the gravel as she pressed a switch. Lucas's vague shadowy shape became reality and she longed for him to come inside with her. Since her parents died she had felt lonely. Even though she had not lived with them exactly she had always known they were there should she need them.

It had been her mother's idea that they convert part of the one wing for her own use. Alina had been for leaving home, finding somewhere of her own. But the arrangement had worked surprisingly well. She had all her home comforts, plus the independence of running her own life, and her mother, to her surprise, had left her strictly alone, only visiting when invited or if something important cropped up.

'I think I'll take a quick check.' Lucas stepped into the hallway.

Alina bristled, wanting him, but not like this. She resented his high-handed manner. 'You have a nerve! I've managed perfectly well up till now. I suggest you go, before I call the police and denounce you as an intruder!'

He stiffened visibly. 'Don't you think you're carrying this hate thing a bit too far? That's three times you've threatened me with the law.'

'No, I don't,' she snapped. She had to lie. No way could she let him know that all the old feelings had come tumbling back, that she loved him, if possible, more desperately than ever before.

'I see.' His eyes were stony, his mouth grim. 'Nevertheless I'll still feel happier once I've checked on your safety. I was going to suggest I stopped the night, but somehow I feel it wouldn't be the right thing to say?'

Behind her back Alina's fingers clenched on the

keys to her car, her heart leapt violently, and she wanted to say, 'Oh, yes. Yes, please, Lucas!' But what she did say was, 'It's a despicable thing to suggest. I thought you'd realised by now that I want nothing to do with you.'

'Then would you consider staying at the Coach House, at my expense, of course, until your affairs are sorted out?'

She eyed him warily, noting with surprise the lines of strain about his mouth, a tired, defeated look in his eyes. Perhaps this new Lucas was unused to women treating him as she had, he certainly did not look too pleased to have his suggestion rejected.

'I'm sorry, the answer is no, and if you still insist on making this ridiculous check please get on with it.'

She remained standing there until he finally returned, then held the door wide, leaving him in no doubt that he was not welcome for one second longer. 'I hope you're satisfied.'

He nodded grimly and disappeared into the darkness without a further word. His engine roared into life as she locked and bolted the door behind him.

Surprisingly Alina felt bereft, her flat unusually empty, and she wished she had not been so quick in turning down his offer.

The house was large enough for him to be no threat to her. Once locked in her wing no one could get in unless they broke down a door—and she would have felt happier with him somewhere within calling distance.

It did not usually bother her, being alone, and now she blamed him for putting uneasy thoughts into her mind. Somehow each little noise sent her into a mild panic, and once in bed she pulled the sheets over her head, staying that way until she fell asleep.

Before opening the shop the next morning she called

on her solicitor with the contract, and he urged her to take Lucas up on it, as she had guessed he would. 'But don't you think it unfair?' she argued.

'All I can see,' he said, 'is that at the end of the day you're likely to receive a sizeable income without having had to do anything for it. I would say you're lucky, if anything.'

What finally made up Alina's mind was a reminder in the post that the insurance was due. And taking into account the valuable furniture and pictures in Wythenhall Manor she knew that she could not afford to lapse it—but neither could she afford to pay it!

She rang the Coach House and spoke to Lucas. 'You've won,' she said quietly, almost in tears. 'Come round and I'll sign,' and then she put down the phone.

Within ten minutes he was there, and it cut her to the quick to see the triumphant smile on his face. 'I knew you'd come to your senses,' he said, as he followed her into the dining hall. 'It was all a matter of time.'

'Necessity,' snapped Alina, 'and you can wipe that smile away, because there are one or two points in the contract that I want to alter.'

'And I say the contract stays as it is or we forget it.' His casual blue knitted shirt clung to his powerful chest, accentuating his immense physical strength. He stood now, arms akimbo, and stared at her deliberately.

Alina held his gaze, fighting her instinctive response to his intense masculinity, knowing that she needed a clear mind to sort out her interests.

But even as she looked into the depths of his dark eyes, felt their power over her, she knew she had lost. A treacherous weakness flooded her limbs and all she wanted to do was walk into his arms and say, 'Look after me, Lucas. I need you.'

Instead she said, 'I don't like the idea of not being involved. After all, this has been my home all my life. What happens to it now is my responsibility, and although I—I'm grateful to you for offering to join me in a partnership, I do feel that—that it would only be fair if I had an equal opportunity in its organisation.'

'My serious little Alina!' Mockery curved his lips. 'Do you really think I'd shoot you down if you so much as set foot outside your own quarters?'

'I—I hope not,' she whispered, her eyes wide as they rested on his face.

A muscle tightened in his jaw. 'Hell, don't look at me like that!' He turned and set the papers out on the table. 'The reason I excluded you from all that will be going on is because I knew that you wouldn't have the time. You have your shop, isn't that enough?'

Away from the mesmerising influence of his eyes Alina was able to say coldly, 'For all the good it is right at this moment I may as well sell.'

'Things are that bad?'

His question had to be purely rhetorical—he must surely know what his grand new showrooms had done to her trade. But she could not stop herself biting. 'They're not only bad, they're impossible, thanks to you. And don't think I don't know why you've done it, although I'm sure less drastic measures would have still done the trick. It was only a matter of time before I'd have had to do something.'

'You're still under the impression that I'm trying to put you out of business?' His voice was suddenly harsh and he looked at her impatiently. 'Hell, Alina, I really had hoped you'd come to your senses.'

She sighed deeply, resignedly. 'Where do you want me to sign?' Why she had thought she could win against him she did not know.

He handed her a gold fountain pen, opening the

document at the appropriate page. When she had finished he added his own signature and stood back, a satisfied smile on his face. Holding out his hand, he said, 'Let's shake on our new partnership. Or maybe a drink would be in order? This is a momentous occasion.'

'To you, maybe,' said Alina quietly, coolly. 'So far as I'm concerned I've just signed my death warrant. And now I must go. I keep the shop open just for the sheer fun of it, did you know that? I love sitting there all day doing nothing.' And it was satisfying to see that her bolt had hit its target.

'I wish you weren't so bitter.' Surprisingly he sounded as though he meant it. 'It won't help our relationship.'

'What relationship?' she tossed angrily. 'So far as I'm concerned the less I see of you the better. Maybe the clause that I keep to my own rooms was a good thing after all. I think I'll abide by it.'

She swung on her heel and gathering up her bag left the house. It was as much his as hers now—more, in fact. He was assuming total responsibility, so he could start by locking up behind them.

But when she drove out of the yard he had still not appeared. It was not difficult to guess that he was already working things out in his mind.

When Alina returned that evening she was astonished to see a couple of vans outside and the sounds of workmen whistling and hammering coming from all corners of the house. Lucas certainly did not believe in wasting time!

She shut herself in her flat, determined to stick to her word and have nothing at all to do with any of this, but when eventually there was silence and the vans had disappeared from in front of the house Alina could not resist taking a look.

They had started at the top. Each bedroom was being completely redecorated. Carpets had been taken up and the valuable furniture carefully covered. And although Alina had presumed that a lick of emulsion would have been Lucas's instruction, tasteful wallpaper was being hung instead. It was all very impressive, but strangely only served to increase her resentment.

Not all the rooms up here had bathrooms, but each had a washbasin and there were two bathrooms and separate toilets along the corridor. On the two floors below each room was en suite, and if he was going to carry on in this vein it would be very luxurious accommodation indeed. She only hoped that the businessmen who came to stay would appreciate their surroundings and take care of the furnishings.

But she was forgetting—it was not her home any longer. She shared it with Lucas. In fact he was entirely responsible for its maintenance and upkeep. It had nothing at all to do with her.

The thought brought tears to her eyes and a lump to her throat. He would never know how hard all this was to take.

It was like having her heritage snatched from beneath her. She hadn't been joking when she had said it was like signing her life away.

Suddenly she could stand it no longer, and raced down to her own flat, closing the door firmly behind her. At least this would stay the same. Nothing would change here.

'Do you approve?'

Lucas's deeply timbred voice came as a shock, and she spun round to find him comfortably seated in an armchair behind the door. 'I guessed it wouldn't take you long to find out what was happening!'

Her eyes blazed brightly, partly from the tears, partly with anger. 'How dare you come in uninvited! The rest of the house might belong to you, but not this flat. It's my personal domain and I don't want you here. Please go!'

'I feel like your company,' he said blandly. 'So if you want to get rid of me you'll have to throw me out.' There was amused defiance on his face as he calmly proceeded to light a cigar.

Alina felt like screaming. Instead she sat stiffly on a high-backed chair in front of the window, remaining resolutely mute, and wondering how long he would be able to put up with her in this frame of mind. Perhaps he would take the hint and go?

She looked outside, at the late evening sun glinting across the trout lake, turning the water to molten gold, at the trees burgeoning into growth, at the fresh spring green everywhere.

Springtime—when new life was born—when she should be happy and delighted that the long winter was over. She should be dancing with joy instead of sitting here fuming, feeling intolerably unhappy, and wishing Lucas on the other side of the world.

She rested her head against the pane and closed her eyes. The next second she was aware of him behind her and stiffened, glancing up sharply.

'It won't always seem this bad.' His voice was soft, cajoling. 'If you'd only unbend and accept me back into your life—as a friend, nothing more—I'm sure everything will seem a lot better.'

'But that's just it,' she snapped. 'I don't want you in my life.' Once he had returned her love. It had been different then. Now it was one-sided, and she was a fool to have even allowed him this close.

His hands rested on her shoulders and she stiffened, wondering what his next move would be. 'I'm here,' he said softly. 'There's not much you can do about it, so why keep fighting?'

Why indeed? Why couldn't everything be as it once was? The answer was simple. Because he had walked out on her! Because he no longer loved her!

'Because there's no point,' she said harshly, shrugging out of his grasp. His touch, though light, had scorched her skin. 'Our life together ended eight years ago, Lucas. Please remember that.'

His lips twisted grimly and he picked up his cigar from the ashtray where it rested. 'You're not likely to let me forget it.' He drew on the cheroot angrily and exhaled a cloud of smoke. 'I had hoped for a pleasant hour, but it seems I was mistaken. I'll go back to the Coach House. Eating alone has become a habit these days.'

Somehow Alina could not let him go. It seemed ridiculous when she had not yet eaten herself. 'I have trout,' she said. 'There's enough for two, if you'd like to join me?'

He looked at her guardedly. 'I don't want your pity.'

'You're not getting it,' she thrust quickly, 'and I shall probably be a pig to you, but if you want to stay you can. I am rather tired, though, and I'd like an early night.'

His smile was wry. 'I've had better invitations, but thank you, yes, I will accept. Can I help?'

'No, thanks.' Working side by side in the kitchen would remind her of what might have been. It would be painful in the extreme.

Lucas sat down. 'Give me a yell if you change your mind.'

Alina felt like closing the kitchen door, but she knew that although he would be out of sight he would not be out of mind. She cleaned and boned the trout and wrapped them in foil with a little stock, placing them in the oven to poach while she boiled potatoes and opened a tin of peas. She made a sauce and when all was ready called out to Lucas.

'I hope eating in the kitchen isn't beneath you these days,' she said, half mocking, half serious.

He frowned. 'You really do think that because my fortunes have changed I too have altered? For heaven's sake, Alina, why can't you accept me? I'm still the same underneath. Nothing there is different.'

Except that you don't love me, she thought bitterly. 'I don't think things will ever be the same again—too much has happened.'

He sat down and picked up his knife and fork, but he did not begin eating straight away. 'You're right, a lot has happened. I feel I've lived a lifetime since leaving Wythenhall. In fact, I might as well admit it, I do feel different. Whereas before I was part of the village, now I feel alienated. People are not so ready to accept me. It's as though my wealth has put up a barrier. I can't understand it. It wasn't a barrier between you and me when you were the one who had the money.'

'Love doesn't take into account minor details like that,' she said caustically. 'But there is a class barrier, without a doubt. My mother didn't approve of our friendship. Yet if she were alive now she'd probably welcome you with open arms. You've gone up in the world, Lucas. The people who were once your friends will be wary of you, they'll feel they're no longer good enough for you.'

'Too true,' he sighed. 'I've looked up the ones who are still here. On the surface they appear friendly, but beneath I feel they resent my success. Do you resent it?'

His blunt question took her by surprise, and when

she did not reply straight away he said, 'Don't bother, the answer's clear.'

Alina did not argue. It seemed pointless. Best leave things as they were. She ate her trout, but it was like sawdust in her mouth and she wished she had not asked him to stay.

Lucas too was tight-faced as he got on with his meal, and when he had finished he said, 'Don't bother about coffee, I'll get one back at the Coach House.' He scraped back his chair and stood up.

Contrarily Alina did not want him to go. The house would seem even more empty than usual. 'It's no trouble,' she said. 'It's already made. Please stay.'

Suspicion filled his eyes as he stared at her darkly. 'What's made you change your mind? A short time ago you gave me strict instructions not to hang around.'

'But I didn't say go without your coffee. Or perhaps you'd prefer a whisky? I found another bottle.' She didn't realise how eager she sounded.

'Later.' Amusement replaced doubt. 'Coffee will do fine right now. Shall we take it into the other room and make ourselves comfortable?'

Alina carried it through on a tray and he placed a small table in front of the settee, leaving her little choice but to sit beside him.

'This is very cosy.' A smile played at the corners of his mouth. 'We must do it more often.'

Alina sipped her coffee, careful to keep several inches between herself and Lucas. 'I didn't realise you would be spending so much time here. Doesn't your work keep you in London?'

He shrugged easily. 'I'm here, there and everywhere. London's my base, but I don't spend much time there. I like to keep my eye on all my different companies. But at the moment this is my baby, and I want to be here to see that things are done properly. I always keep an eye on new projects—I don't believe in delegating work I can do myself.'

His confidence amazed Alina anew. 'You keep your fingers on every pulse? Very admirable. How did you start?'

He smiled. 'I wondered when that question would come. Are you really interested, Alina?'

'I wouldn't have asked otherwise,' she retorted swiftly, and then on a softer note, 'Yes, Lucas, I really would like to know. I often wondered what had happened to you.'

'And me you, my love.'

Her head jerked swiftly at the anguished tone in his voice, and somehow she found herself caught up in his arms.

Desire burned in his eyes, and with an aching groan he gathered her close, his mouth finding hers hungrily. She had no thought to resist. Of their own volition her arms crept behind his neck, her fingers trembling as they threaded through his strong golden hair.

His kiss was deep and passionate and more urgent than she had ever remembered, as though he intended catching up on all the years. A moan escaped Alina as her head sank back and his lips burned a trail down the column of her throat, his hand gently caressing her breast.

But somewhere in the depths of her passion she remembered what he had done to her. She must put a stop to this foolishness—and soon—or all would be lost.

CHAPTER FOUR

WITH an effort Alina pulled out of Lucas's arms, her face flushed, her eyes brilliant. 'You swine! Keep your hands off me. I invited you for a meal, nothing else. If I'd known this was what you had in mind I'd have made sure you never set foot inside.'

Lucas's lips twisted cynically. 'Don't come that with me! Your response was instinctive. Why the sudden withdrawal? Can you deny that you don't want me?'

Alina stared at him, almost hating him. He sounded so confident, so sure that she was willing to fall into his arms, to take up again where they had left off. 'My wanting you has been dead a long time. I—I thought you were kissing me as a thank-you for the meal. I never dreamt it would develop into anything else, or I would certainly not have let you touch me.'

'And you expect me to believe that?' His dark eyes were intent as they rested upon her face. 'What sort of an idiot do you take me for?'

Alina turned away, afraid he might read the truth. He had always been good at knowing what she was thinking. He used to accuse her of wearing her heart on her sleeve and at that time she had been amused by it, now she wished desperately she had the ability to hide her feelings behind a mask of indifference.

'I think it's time you went,' she said tightly.

'Before you give yourself away altogether?' A humourless smile curved his lips. 'I don't know what you're afraid of, Alina, and I've given up trying to understand you.'

She glared impatiently. 'It's simple. I don't love you

any more, and I have a rule never to allow myself to become involved with a man I don't love.'

His eyes narrowed. 'Exactly when did you stop loving me?'

She sensed that the answer was important to him, though what difference it made now she could not imagine. 'It should be obvious,' she retorted. 'I can give you the date if you like. I was just sixteen, and I think it was the unhappiest birthday I've ever spent.'

'And did it happen just like that, your falling out of love with me?' He had risen and stood looking down at her, his face now a picture of conflicting emotions.

Alina nodded. 'Surprising, isn't it?'

'Bloody incredible,' he snarled. 'You're right, it is time I left. I'll try not to force myself on you again.' He picked up his coat and slung it over one shoulder. Grim lines tautened his jaw. 'It's stupid, I know, but I thought that perhaps there was something left of what we once had going for us. I must be more of a fool than I realised.'

Tears stung the back of Alina's eyes as the door closed none too quietly behind him. So he had hoped to gather up the remnants of their relationship? But if he still cared for her, why had he gone in the first place?

She could only presume that he had decided he did not want to be tied down, that he had wanted to see something of the world before getting married. But if he had told her, she would have understood, she would have let him go. They could have postponed the wedding until he felt ready for it.

Or would she have accepted it that easily? In her early teens she had been very emotional, and would have more than likely flown into hysterics had he even hinted at such a thing. Perhaps this was what he had been afraid of? Perhaps he thought that under the circumstances he had done the kindest thing?

But for whatever reason she had no wish to become entangled again. Who knew how many more hearts he had broken? There must have been a few. He was damnably attractive, too much so for her peace of mind.

With a dull ache throbbing in her temples Alina took the tray through to the kitchen and washed up slowly. She felt very bitter towards Lucas right at this moment and wished with all her heart that it had not been necessary to involve him with Wythenhall Manor. If only there had been some other solution!

But there hadn't. She was stuck with him whether she liked it or not. All she could hope was that he would keep out of her way.

She left for the shop extra early the next morning, before the workmen came, before Lucas. She did not think she could bear to face him again for a while.

Towards dinnertime the doorbell jangled and Alina looked up in surprise. She had got so used to sitting there all day doing nothing that it was quite a novelty to think she might have a customer.

The woman was a stranger to her, although Alina had the feeling that she had seen her somewhere before. She watched her as she browsed and it occurred to her that this plump middle-aged person was not really interested in buying. She was here for some other reason.

Then she remembered. It was the woman in the café who had been talking to Mrs Smith. Alina felt her hackles rise. 'Were you interested in anything special?' she asked crisply. 'A reproduction claiming to be a genuine antique, perhaps?'

The woman's podgy face flushed, and she avoided Alina's eyes. 'I—I wanted to——'

'To assure yourself that the lies you've been spreading are true? Perhaps you wouldn't mind telling me where you got your information from? I don't take kindly to having my reputation ruined.'

Shaking her head, the woman sat down heavily, her flush deepened to an ugly red. 'Please—let me speak.'

Alina folded her arms and said impatiently, 'Feel free, although I think you've said quite enough to be going on with.'

'It was all a mistake,' she began hurriedly. 'A—a friend of mine bought a chiffonier off you and I had one exactly like it. Mine was a reproduction, I knew, I couldn't afford the real thing, but they looked identical.'

'Did she have it examined by an expert?' asked Alina sharply.

The woman shook her head. 'But I have since.'

'Don't you think it would have been the obvious thing to do in the first place, before spreading lies? You've ruined my business, do you know that.' Alina was not quite sure whether she believed the woman. Oh, she believed she had started the rumours, all right, but she was not so sure about her reason for it. Lucas Delgado had to fit into this somewhere.

'Do you know Mr Delgado?' she asked suddenly, hoping to shock the woman into admission.

One glance at her face revealed that she did indeed know him. Alina felt her heart plummet and supposed that deep down she had been hoping the woman spoke the truth.

'He's a nice gentleman,' admitted the woman. 'We met in the Coach House. I do some cleaning there. I heard that he knew quite a lot about antiques, and I asked him if he would have a look at my friend's chiffonier.'

'And he confirmed that it was genuine?'

She nodded. 'And he suggested that I come to you to apologise. He said that he too had heard someone had been trying to put you out of business by spreading unfounded tales, and he said he felt sorry for you and that something should be done about it. Is he a friend of yours?'

Alina shook her head. That was a turn-up for the book—Lucas sorry for her! 'Not a friend, a business acquaintance. I'm surprised he's bothered about me.' In fact she was more than surprised. She was astounded. For the first time she smiled at the woman. 'I do appreciate you telling me this. You must have found it very hard.' But not as hard as she would find it apologising to Lucas! 'Try and make sure that everyone else you've spoken to knows it too, will you? Then perhaps trade will pick up and I won't have to close down.'

Shock crossed the woman's face. 'Did I do that to you? Oh, lord, I never imagined. No wonder you were angry! I'm so sorry. I——'

Alina took her hands gently. 'It wasn't only that. Please—don't distress yourself. I'll survive, I know I will.'

'I hope so, I really do.' There was genuine concern on the woman's face now. 'I'll never forgive myself if you have to close. I never realised how a thing like this can snowball. I'd never have said anything, if I'd known.'

'I'm sure you wouldn't.' Alina began to feel quite sorry for her. 'Would you like a cup of tea?'

An hour later they were the best of friends and Mrs Plant, or Flo, as she preferred to be called, assured Alina that she would put in a word for her wherever she could. 'I know a lot of people in high places,' she said proudly, 'and they're all on this antique lark. I'll tell them about you.'

'I expect they would prefer somewhere like Mr Delgado's new shop in Cheltenham,' said Alina wryly.

Flo touched her arm. 'Don't you believe it! It's the service that counts. You have a nice little place here and some lovely stuff. I wish I could afford it myself. Now I must go.'

Alina felt drained. It had been an unexpected turn of events, and now she was left with the task of facing Lucas—and apologising. It would be the hardest thing she had ever had to do—especially after the way she had spoken to him last night.

But there was no getting out of it. After all, he had intervened on her behalf and she ought to be grateful. Well, she was really, but it was still not going to be an easy thing to do.

Two weeks went by without her seeing Lucas. They were long lonely weeks. Alina wanted him more desperately than she cared to admit, and she sometimes wished she hadn't been so hasty in telling him that his attentions were not welcome.

Each evening after the workmen had gone she toured the house, inspecting the work, begrudgingly admiring. Certainly no expense was being spared.

But deep down she hoped she might meet Lucas accidentally. She still had the onerous task of apologising for mistrusting him, but it was worth that just for the sake of seeing him, talking to him, dreaming a little about what might have been.

Business picked up slightly and that helped, and through the grapevine she heard that the prices in Lucas's shop in Cheltenham were also being gradually increased. This made her angry. It proved conclusively that he had done it purely to force her hand—and now that he had got what he wanted he was asking more realistic prices.

'I thought it was too good to be true,' grumbled one of the villagers who in the past had often called in on Alina to see what she had new, but who had been conspicuous by her absence since the new shop opened.

Most of Alina's stuff was small—she had none of the large pieces of furniture that Lucas's shop boasted—for one thing she hadn't the room, for another her customers could never afford this type of thing. She specialised in silver and jewellery, and had a good selection of clocks and china and pictures, and what with her faithful regulars and the passing holiday trade she managed to make a fair living.

'And I tell you what else,' continued the woman. 'He won't go out of his way to get you anything—not like you. If it's not in stock he'll say sorry and good day.'

Alina smiled. She had made her reputation by always agreeing to search for anything she had not got—and usually she was lucky. She attended numerous sales every month and had a keen eye for what would or would not be of interest to her customers.

It was satisfying to know that her reputation had not been ruined after all, neither by Flo's hastily spoken words, or Lucas's undercutting tactics.

Flo popped in regularly to pass the time of day and mentioned quite innocently that Mr Delgado had checked out. 'I believe he's gone abroad,' she said, unaware of the impact of her words. 'But I expect you know that, you being in business together?'

Word had somehow leaked that he now had a vested interest in Wythenhall Manor and that it was going to be turned into a conference centre. Alina had lost count of the number of people who had spoken to her about it—some thinking it the best thing that could happen to her—others afraid that their village might be ruined.

She smiled at Flo. 'He comes and goes,' she said airily. 'You never know where he's going to be next. Did he say when he'd be back?'

'Not that I know of,' admitted the little woman. 'But I can find out.'

And she would. She was the type of woman who knew everyone's business as well as her own. Alina shook her head. 'It's all right. I expect he'll be in touch.'

But knowing that there was no likelihood of a chance meeting now made Alina even more despondent. She tried going to bed early, but she could not sleep, and this only made it worse. Lucas dominated her thoughts hopelessly.

And then the reliable Flo informed her that he had returned with an attractive redhead in tow! 'I was just going off work when they came,' she explained. 'You should have seen her luggage—real leather! And the way she clung to Mr Delgado's arm, her big eyes shining like jewels, I shouldn't wonder whether they aren't engaged or something!'

Alina thought her heart had stopped beating, she felt faint and her face drained of colour, but even to her own ears her voice sounded remarkably steady when she replied. 'It will be nice for him to have company. He knows no one here—all the friends he grew up with have left.' And he didn't want her! She had long ago given up all idea of that. He had merely been testing her, trying to see what sort of reaction he would get after all these years.

And now he knew—he was steering clear. She guessed any further contact would be purely on a business level. But it was sheer hell knowing that he was with another woman. She wondered whether he had done this deliberately, because of the way she, Alina, had treated him, or whether this unknown redhead was in fact an old friend whom he could not bear to be parted from.

Her own situation became more difficult until she found herself unwilling to return home each evening in case she bumped into them. It was silly and pointless, she knew, but there was nothing she could do about it. The saying, 'Absence makes the heart grow fonder,' was certainly true in her case. She loved Lucas desperately, and although she had once thought her heart mended she discovered not a very good job had been done on it. Already it was showing signs of breaking yet again.

And whether it was because she was feeling low, or whether it was one of those things, Alina managed to pick up a 'flu bug that was running riot through the village. All morning she sneezed and shivered, and by lunchtime decided that there was nothing for it but to shut the shop and go home. Even the girl who normally helped her out had 'flu.

To make matters worse Lucas's car was in the courtyard. If she hadn't been feeling so ill she would have turned tail and run, even though it was stupid because after all it was her own home. All she could hope that she could creep in unnoticed.

She garaged her Mini and made her way round the back where there was less chance of them meeting. Her legs felt distinctly wobbly as she pushed open the heavy oak door, turning immediately to climb the spiralling stone steps which were rarely used, but which led to the first floor and subsequently her flat.

Halfway up she wondered whether she would make it. She had never felt so ill in her life. She sat down for a moment, feeling the stone strike chill into her limbs while at the same time her body was bathed in perspiration.

With a tremendous effort she forced herself to continue, only to find when she got to the top that the door was bolted from the other side. Then she remembered that she had done it with the express purpose of keeping Lucas out!

She could have cried. Normally it wasn't fastened—there had never been any reason. Now she had no alternative but to go back down and re-enter the front way as she normally did.

It was the bottom step that did it. Well worn over the centuries, it had always been tricky, and Alina in her present weakened state forgot to be careful. Her ankle turned and she fell, crying out as her head hit the flagged stone floor.

It could have been no more than a few seconds that she lay there, yet it felt like hours, the pain that was filling her head adding to her other aches and disorders, and she did not even seem to have the strength to pick herself up.

A moment or two later Lucas appeared, towering over her, glowering angrily. 'What the hell are you playing at? You could have got yourself killed!'

Trust him to have no sympathy! Tears filled her eyes and to her horror rolled down her cheeks. 'I make a habit of falling down steps,' she cried weakly. 'Go away, I'm all right.'

With a supreme effort she pushed herself up, but was unable to stop herself wincing as the pain in her head increased. She touched her brow and felt it swelling already.

Frowning harshly, Lucas swept back her hair, inspecting the bruised skin, noting the shine of sweat, and, for the first time, her pallor. 'Are you ill?'

''Flu.' Her mouth felt dry now and she knew that any second she would collapse again.

He swore loudly and swept her up into his arms before she could even attempt to argue. It was then that Alina saw the girl behind him. Flo had not exaggerated when she had said she was beautiful.

Gleaming copper hair framed a face that was so perfect it was unbelievable. Brilliant emerald eyes were fixed firmly upon Alina, their oval shape emphasised by thick curling lashes and a touch of brown shadow. Clear gloss made her lips look soft and moist, and even in the midst of her pain Alina wondered whether Lucas found them kissable.

The thought was disquieting. The girl also had an incredible tan, making Alina wonder whether the two of them had been away together.

She closed her eyes, unwilling to look any more at the girl who was apparently as much a part of Lucas's life as she herself had once been, and felt herself being carried back out of the house and round towards the other entrance.

For a mad moment in his arms it was easy to pretend that nothing had changed. Despite the fact that she felt so ill it did not stop her heart racing. Contact between her and Lucas was explosive.

All too soon, it seemed, he deposited her on the bed. 'Vanessa, my dear, help Alina get undressed.'

Alina did not want this other girl's help, but by this stage she felt so weak there was nothing for it but to submit to her attentions.

Vanessa was efficient, briskly stripping off her damp clothes, asking whether she wanted a towel to dry herself—which Alina refused—and hustling a cotton nightie over her head.

She did not speak once during the whole performance, only when Alina was lying safely beneath the sheets did she say, 'So you're Alina!' and it was as though she knew all about her, but strangely did not resent her. 'Lucas told me about your problem. I think if I were you I would have sold up altogether and found myself a nice little house.'

Alina felt too weak to argue. 'I like it here,' she managed. 'It's been my home all my life.'

Vanessa nodded sympathetically. 'Lucas said something about working here when he was a lad. And didn't you have a crush on him?' A frown marred her smooth brow for a moment. 'Isn't it funny what we do when we're kids? I remember once having a crush on someone, I thought he was fabulous. Now I can't stand the sight of him. I expect it's the same with you and Lucas?'

Alina gave a wobbly smile. 'He's altered. He's not at all the same person.' And how dared he discuss their personal relationship with a complete stranger!

'And you preferred him as he was, you poor dear?' Vanessa shrugged matter of factly. 'That's life, isn't it? Have you a boy-friend at the moment?'

But before Alina could answer Lucas came in. 'I'm sure Alina doesn't feel like talking,' he said crisply.

Vanessa shot him a wounded look. 'I was just being friendly!'

He smiled, his face relaxing. 'I'm sure you were.'

A look of understanding passed between the two of them, making Alina feel sicker than she already was. She closed her eyes and said weakly, 'I'd like to be alone—if you wouldn't mind.'

Lucas nodded. 'The doctor will be here shortly. I took the liberty of phoning him.'

'It wasn't necessary,' she demurred, 'it's only 'flu,' but her argument carried no conviction. Lucas was in command now and he would do whatever he felt right.

She closed her eyes, not opening them again until

they had gone. Vanessa's husky voice, low and intimate, carried up to her. 'How ill the poor girl looks! It's lucky I'm here, I'll be able to look after her.'

And Lucas's response. 'Darling Vanessa, you're wonderful. Are you sure you won't mind?'

'For you, Lucas, anything.'

Their voices faded after that, and Alina was left alone with her aches and pains—and her misery! Lucas had a nerve bringing that girl here! What was he trying to prove, that he didn't care that she had rejected him? Was he emphasising the fact that there were plenty more girls interested in him? Or was Vanessa really someone special? There had certainly been a rapport between them that did not happen overnight.

But she did really feel too ill even to worry about Lucas's girl-friends. It was inevitable that a man as attractive as he would have plenty—except that she wished he had kept them away from here.

She drifted into a light sleep when the doctor arrived. He confirmed that she did indeed have 'flu and ordered her to stay in bed for at least a week.

She had was appalled. 'A week! I thought a couple of days and I'd be all right. How about my shop?'

He smiled. He had known Alina since she was a baby. 'It will be waiting, don't fret yourself about it.'

But Alina did worry. She couldn't afford to keep it closed. 'The man's an idiot,' she said to Vanessa, who had hovered while he examined her.

'He knows his job,' said Vanessa firmly. 'I'll pop into the village with your prescription. Is there anything else you want?'

Alina shook her head, hating Vanessa for being so nice and understanding. She didn't want to like Lucas's friend; she wanted to resent her. But when the girl was putting herself out for a perfect stranger, and quite willingly too, there was no way that she could condemn her.

It did not take the redhaired girl long. In less than half an hour she was back with the medicine and tablets. She dosed Alina as one would a child. 'Do you want anything to eat?' she asked afterwards.

Alina shook her head, only to find that it hurt considerably. Her lump felt the size of an egg, but the doctor had said there was no damage, merely prescribing tablets for the pain.

'Then try to sleep,' said Vanessa, smiling warmly. 'I'll go and find Lucas. He must think I've deserted him.'

The next few days were a confused blur in Alina's mind. She was aware of Vanessa administering the medicine, bathing her, stripping off sweat-soaked clothes and getting her into warm clean ones. She could not recall seeing Lucas. Perhaps he didn't like illness? It was funny, she had once thought she knew him so well, but this was one thing she did not know about him.

With her strength returning Alina began to fret about the shop. 'I'll have to get up soon,' she said to Vanessa. 'I'm losing trade. I can't keep the shop closed indefinitely.'

Vanessa's beautiful lips curved into a secretive smile. 'It's all been taken care of. Lucas has put someone in to look after it for you. In fact he said business has been quite good under the circumstances.'

Alina bristled. 'Who? Who's he put in?'

'Someone from London, I think,' shrugged Vanessa. 'I'm not really sure.'

'London?' Alina was appalled. 'I'm quite sure the hard-selling tactics they use there are not the same as I employ here. He'll put me out of business—if he hasn't already. My customers are very special, I treat each one as a friend. We have an understanding.'

Surprised by Alina's strong reaction, Vanessa said confidently, 'I'm sure you've misjudged Lucas. He wouldn't want to put you out of business.'

Wouldn't he? thought Alina. That's all you know. If Vanessa thought he was so perfect then she was the one who was doing the misjudging.

'I want to speak to him,' she said firmly. 'Send him up, will you—and Vanessa, leave us alone.' She had no wish for this outsider to hear her and Lucas arguing.

It was well over an hour before Lucas finally came to her room. Alina had grown more furious by the minute, wondering whether he was deliberately keeping her waiting. Surely he couldn't be all that busy?

He stood just inside the doorway, as devastating as ever, wearing tight jeans and a sloppy sweater. There was a smudge of dust on his brow and his fair hair was untidy. He looked as though he had been working, though why, when he could afford to pay an army of men, she had no idea.

His brown eyes rested on her face. 'How are you feeling? Vanessa tells me you've been asking about the shop, so I guess you're much better.'

'For all the interest you've taken I could be dead!' Alina shot back testily.

Dark brows rose, and he smiled cynically. 'You've missed me, then? But to keep the records straight Vanessa has kept me informed. I simply thought you wouldn't want me hanging around in the state you were in—and judging by the look on your face now I'm not about to receive your thanks for keeping things ticking over in your absence.'

'I'd have preferred it if you'd kept your nose out of my affairs!'

'My, you are feeling better! As I understand it, you've hardly had the strength to speak these last few days. What have you been doing, saving it up for me?' He moved closer to the bed, thumbs hooked casually through his belt, distinct amusement on his face.

Alina tossed her head savagely. 'I've only just found out what you've done. You had no right installing someone in my shop without telling me! Heaven knows what harm you've done—you and your high-falutin' fancy fellows from London. I saw enough of that one in Cheltenham to know the type you pick.'

'It's not a fellow, it's a woman,' said Lucas, and his voice had become dangerously quiet. 'She knows a lot about antiques and she's doing very well, so you should be thankful.'

'Well, I'm not,' snapped Alina, 'and I'm surprised that you've even bothered. Wouldn't it have been a perfect opportunity to let my shop run down altogether?'

He followed her line of thought perfectly. 'So that you wouldn't be able to pay your rent and I'd chuck you out—and maybe throw in a takeover bid at the same time?' A muscle tightened in his jaw as he clenched his teeth angrily. 'Hell, Alina, what sort of person do you take me for?'

'You're ruthless, and so far as I can see you wouldn't help out anyone—unless the advantages were all on your side.' Alina glared ebulliently, even though she knew she was in danger of losing this battle.

'And how could keeping your shop going help me? Answer me that, will you?'

He looked taller than ever standing over her bed, and Alina felt weak and defenceless and suddenly realised how stupid she had been to start all this.

'Because it just might be in your mind to take over that as well,' she blurted. 'One foot in the door and the rest should be easy. Is that it?'

He snapped a fist into the palm of his other hand. 'Of all the bloody infuriating women I've ever met, you're the worst! Goddammit, Alina, I thought you were my friend. What am I going to do with you?'

Alina tucked in her chin and looked at him demurely through her lashes. 'Would you mind not swearing in front of me, Lucas? I'm not used to it.'

Mockery lifted his brows. 'I've heard you do your share. But I never was a one for fine language, and I'm sure as hell not going to change now.'

'So money hasn't changed that side of you?' Though she was certain she could not remember him swearing so violently in the past. Perhaps he had been on his best behaviour when he was working for her parents.

'So far as I'm aware I've not changed at all, except to get richer,' he snarled. 'It's you who's done the changing. You're a different woman entirely.'

Swift colour flared in Alina's cheeks. 'Are you congratulating yourself on getting rid of me before we took those final vows?'

'Maybe,' he shrugged. 'I don't reckon it would have lasted. I rather suspect we'd have been divorced by now.'

His harsh utterly unexpected words crucified Alina. She drew in a swift breath and slid beneath the sheets, pulling them over her face, fighting devastating tears that were forcing their way to the surface.

'That's right,' he sneered, 'hide! Run away and bury your head in the sand. Take the easy way out. You should be good at it by now!'

Then the door slammed and there was silence.

CHAPTER FIVE

LUCAS'S strange remark puzzled Alina, so much that she forgot her tears and struggled to a sitting position, staring at the door as though by so doing she could call him back and ask him to explain himself.

What should she be good at? It was a riddle, a complete and utter riddle, and she was still trying to work it out when Vanessa returned. And the redhead didn't look too happy either. 'What have you done to Lucas?' she demanded. 'He's just bitten my head off.'

'You should be so lucky,' returned Alina irritably. 'He's just about destroyed me.'

Vanessa looked at her keenly. 'Want to talk about it?'

To a current girl-friend? She must be joking! Alina shook her head. 'No, thanks, it's kind of private.'

Vanessa looked as though she thought the pair of them insane. 'Well, whatever it is it must be pretty bad. I've never known him in such a foul mood. In fact I've never known him in any sort of mood. He's the most even-tempered man I've ever met.'

'Then you can't have known him very long,' said Alina.

'Or perhaps it's because we're in love,' said Vanessa quietly. 'I don't think it will be long before he asks me to marry him. It's a pity he's turning this place into a conference centre. I really would enjoy living here.'

For the second time in as many minutes Alina felt devastated, and ready to scratch Vanessa's eyes out. Quite how she managed it she didn't know, but somehow she summoned up a smile. 'You must let me

76

know when congratulations are in order. And if you wouldn't mind, I'd like to get some sleep. I feel quite drained after all the—excitement.'

But in fact she had never been so wide-awake in her life. Two such shocks were more than she could stand in one day. Vanessa and Lucas in love! She had guessed that, but she had never dreamt that they were contemplating marriage.

It made her realise that deep down she had been hoping for a reconciliation. Now it was painfully obvious that it was out of the question. Lucas had been curious to see whether any spark of her old love was left, that was all, and he must have been relieved. Otherwise it could have been embarrassing to turn up here with Vanessa and have her confronted by his old and still obviously infatuated lover.

But what hurt equally, or perhaps even more, was his suggestion that their own marriage would never have worked. There had been no doubt in her mind, even though she was barely sixteen. She had known what she wanted then—and she still felt the same now.

Lucas was the one who had had the change of heart, despite trying to lay the blame on her, and right at this very moment she wished she could hate him, she wished she could say, 'Marry Vanessa and the best of British. She's welcome to you!'

But love was unkind. It hurt like hell picturing him with the copper-haired beauty. Theirs, hers and Lucas's, had been a perfect relationship. Why couldn't it have lasted? Exactly why had he turned chicken and run? It was a question she was unlikely to get answered. Why does anyone fall out of love?

It was another two hours before Vanessa returned, opening the door softly and poking her head round. 'Ah, you're awake.' She smiled, a wide friendly smile, and she looked happy. Presumably Lucas had got over his foul mood. How Alina wished they could get over their differences so easily!

'I've fixed you some food. Are you ready for it?' Vanessa came into the room bearing a tray. 'It's not much—soup and a chicken omelette. I thought it might tempt you.'

Alina had eaten hardly anything during her illness, but now she felt hungry. 'Mm, lovely,' she said, smiling in return. 'I really am sorry to keep putting you to so much trouble.'

Vanessa settled the tray across Alina's knees. 'No trouble at all. I cook for Lucas anyway. He's always starving.' She sat down, prepared to wait while Alina ate. 'I must say what a marvellous kitchen you have downstairs. It's a pleasure to work in. And the bedrooms are a dream. I'm in that one with the fourposter bed. It's so romantic. It will be quite a comedown when I have to move up.'

Alina was not quite sure that she followed all this. 'I thought you were at the Coach House? You and Lucas?'

Vanessa's musical laugh came quickly. 'Didn't you know? As soon as you were taken ill we moved in here. It seemed the obvious thing to do.'

Alina's spoon rested in her soup. She suddenly felt that she could drink no more. It must have been because of her illness that she had never realised, but now she thought about it, it should have been obvious. Vanessa had been constantly on hand to look after her, and Alina herself had hardly known day from night in those first days.

But for them to move in! Were they sleeping together? The thought was like a knife in her side. She quickly asked her next question. 'What do you mean, when you move upstairs? Haven't you a home of your own?'

Again Vanessa laughed. 'Typical Lucas not to tell you anything! I'm going to work here—receptionist-cum-secretary.'

'Oh!' It was all Alina could manage. 'Does that mean Lucas will be spending a lot of his time here too?'

Vanessa tossed her copper waves and smiled prettily. 'I certainly hope so.'

Alina attempted another spoonful of soup. She liked Vanessa, she really did. She was an open, friendly, considerate girl, and she and Lucas were admirably suited, but she did not think she could survive the constant pressure of seeing the two of them together.

The ache around her heart became a physical pain and she closed her eyes, so that Vanessa would not see her anguish.

'What I can't understand,' continued Vanessa, 'is why you aren't involved more in all this. After all, it was your home—still is in one respect. Aren't you interested in what's happening to it?'

Alina looked at her, her eyes blank now, tempted to tell her that Lucas himself had imposed the ban. But it seemed cruel to reveal this other side of Lucas when Vanessa saw him only through rose-coloured spectacles. One day she would find out for herself.

'I have my shop,' she said. 'That in itself is a full-time job. I wouldn't have time to participate in the running of the conference centre as well.'

'Of course.' Vanessa nodded as though understanding. 'Finish your soup before it gets cold.'

But she didn't understand; she wouldn't in a thousand years. Alina sometimes wondered whether she understood things herself. Her whole life had become one painful puzzle. She could no longer fathom Lucas out. From the uncomplicated person she had known he had become an enigma. He was again a part of her life, yet at the same time he wasn't. He was there, but he was untouchable. They had no relationship, except from a distance.

It became all at once imperative that she get better quickly. She had to go back to work, she had to move out of this house where he was here every day with Vanessa, where she had nothing to do but lie and think and torture herself with the thought of them together.

She finished her soup and began her omelette. It was superb, she had to admit. Vanessa was a good cook—she would make Lucas a good wife.

A piece of chicken suddenly stuck in her throat. There she was again, marrying them off in her mind! Oh, God, how was she going to stand up to it all?

Seeing her cough, Vanessa got up and handed her a glass of milk. 'Did I leave a bone in?' she quipped, and she was so natural and so charming that Alina felt a traitor for harbouring anything but nice thoughts about her.

When she had finished her supper, Vanessa took her tray. 'Shall I come back and sit with you? Now you're feeling better I expect you're lonely. I'll bring Lucas too. He can tell you all about the work that's been done. I expect you're dying to know.'

Without giving Alina a chance to agree she left the room. Alina felt like yelling after her, 'For God's sake don't bring Lucas here!' She could stand Vanessa on her own, or Lucas, but the two of them together? That really was piling on the agony.

Perhaps she could pretend to be asleep? She snuggled down between the sheets, turning her back to the door, but they came in laughing and chattering so loudly that had she really been asleep they would have woken her.

'Oh, I'm sorry,' apologised Vanessa. 'Are you tired, would you rather we left you alone?'

Alina opened her eyes, saw only Lucas's giant figure standing over her, and said, 'Not at all—sit down, stay as long as you like.'

He was smiling, a deeply sensual smile, but she knew that it was left over from Vanessa. It was not intended for her. Nevertheless it made her tremble and she was glad of the protective bedclothes.

He moved away and the two of them sat side by side on the window seat. Lucas's arm rested along the back, and although Vanessa was not desperately close it looked like a caress, as though he wanted nothing more than to pull her against him, and Alina felt sick, and wondered whether she would be able to get through the whole evening without giving herself away.

'Tell her the good news,' said Vanessa, laughing into Lucas's eyes, their heads close.

Silver and copper! The two went well together. Unbidden as always the thought came into Alina's mind. How she wished she could stop classing them as a pair.

'I'm not sure that she's well enough to hear it.' His deeply timbred voice mocked her. 'Are you, Alina? It might be a shock, or on the other hand it might be a pleasant surprise.'

'Unless you tell me I'll never find out.' She amazed herself by the lightness of her tone, and pushing herself up pulled a knitted jacket about her shoulders. She felt cold, although the central heating was on.

It was Lucas's presence that did it. A chill struck her heart whenever she thought of him—him and Vanessa—together! A whole lifetime of being together! Oh, she must stop torturing herself like this.

'We open in a week,' he announced cheerfully.

'So soon?' Alina was indeed shocked. 'How did you manage it?'

'Everyone will work hard—for a price. I paid the men well—and they served me well. Adverts have gone in all the trade journals and various other places where they should be seen by the right people. Naturally we'll be quiet to start with. We have to get known. People need time to arrange their seminars or conventions or whatever. But we must be ready. They'll want to come and see for themselves what facilities we have to offer. I've ordered brochures, they should be here in a day or two.'

Alina was speechless. She had never dreamt that it would all be ready so soon. He really had organised everything incredibly well. She ought to be congratulating him.

Instead she felt like crying. Wythenhall Manor was no longer a home. In a comparatively short space of time it had been transformed into an impersonal business centre. But equally painful was the fact that she herself had not been involved. She could understand Vanessa's curiosity about this. It must have seemed a very peculiar arrangement.

'Well, aren't you going to say anything?' Lucas's full attention was upon her.

'I'm impressed,' she said flatly.

Catching her expression, Vanessa said, 'I think she's disappointed because she's had no hand in it. Trust you to catch 'flu at the wrong time, Alina!'

'Alina wouldn't have participated anyway,' said Lucas coldly. 'This side of the arrangement has nothing to do with her.'

'But why?' argued Vanessa. 'It's her house. I was asking her the same thing earlier. I think it's grossly unfair. I know I'd want a say in it if it was me.'

'You're different,' he snapped. 'Alina's shop takes up all her time. I'm doing her a favour by taking this place off her hands.'

Is that what he thought? Alina's lips compressed and she bit back an angry retort. Her arguments with Lucas were not for Vanessa's ears.

'Well, I think you're an old meanie.' Vanessa laughed at him as she spoke. 'You want to take all the credit, I know.' And then to Alina, 'He loves getting involved in setting up new businesses, he has quite a flair for it. But once they've got going he'll either sell them at a huge profit or just put in an appearance every now and then.'

She seemed to know a lot about him. Alina wondered how they had met, how long they had been friends, and it was difficult not to resent Vanessa's intimate knowledge.

Trying to match Vanessa's light tone, she said, 'I hope he doesn't try to sell this place, or I'll be after his blood!'

'I don't think he'll do that.' Vanessa looked at him tenderly. 'You have a soft spot for Wythenhall Manor too, haven't you, darling?'

He was suddenly angry no longer. 'Hey, don't give my secrets away! This is Alina's first love, you'll make her jealous.'

'Alina's not that sort,' said Vanessa.

Their gentle mockery, their perfect understanding, made Alina turn her head away swiftly. This was punishment in the extreme.

'Is something wrong?'

She had been unaware that Lucas had seen the fleeting pain before she moved. 'It's my head,' she lied, smoothing her hand over her brow where the bruise had turned a yellowish purple. 'It still hurts sometimes.'

'Perhaps you're overdoing it? I think we ought to leave, Vanessa, let her get some sleep. I knew it wasn't a very good idea of yours coming up here like this.' He

stood up, pulling his companion after him—and Alina
noticed that he did not let go her hand.

So it had been with reluctance that he had visited
her! And now he couldn't wait to get Vanessa on her
own. Before her face gave her away altogether she
slid back down between the sheets. 'It's silly how
tired I get these days,' she mumbled. 'I can't
understand it.'

''Flu does that to you.' Vanessa tucked the sheets
more closely about her. 'I'll pop in before we go to
bed—in case you're still awake and want something.
Goodnight for now.'

From the doorway Lucas too called goodnight. He
looked as though he was impatient to leave.

Alina felt bitter and unhappy and had to fight back
self-pitying tears. Although her flat was an integral
part of the house she felt completely cut off. Once the
door was shut she could hear no sound and had no
way of knowing what they were doing.

Vanessa had said, when *we* go to bed! Did that mean
what Alina thought it meant? Or was she being
spiteful and interpreting things wrongly? It would be
nice to think so, but Vanessa had that aura about her
of a woman whose desires were about to be satisfied.
Alina knew exactly how she felt. She had once been
that way with Lucas herself.

True to her word, Vanessa did look in later, but
Alina pretended to be asleep. She did not want to face
the other woman again tonight, she was afraid of what
she might see.

But so tormented was she by thoughts of Vanessa
and Lucas that she did not sleep at all. When dawn
came she felt a wreck and began to wonder whether
her 'flu wasn't going to turn into something else.

Vanessa expressed concern when she brought in her
breakfast tray. 'My word, Alina, whatever's wrong?

You look awful! Are you worse? Shall I send for the doctor again?'

Alina managed a weak smile. 'I've had a bad night, that's all. A cup of tea will revive me, and then I think I'll get up.'

'Oh, no, you won't. Heavens, we don't want a relapse!' Vanessa put down the tray and poured Alina's tea, bringing it over and sitting on the edge of the bed, her green eyes anxious.

'But I can't stay here for ever,' argued Alina. 'I've put you to enough trouble already. You didn't come here to play nursemaid.'

Vanessa shrugged. 'Who cares, I'm getting paid for it. Besides, it makes a change. I'm quite enjoying myself.'

Alina, who had been about to sip her tea, put the cup down unsteadily. 'Getting paid? I don't follow?'

'I'm Lucas's P.A., didn't you know?' She laughed incredulously. 'Heavens, that man! At least that's my official title. I'm more like a Girl Friday, wet nurse and a slave all rolled into one. I do whatever he asks me to do, and if that means looking after you, then that's what I do.'

'But you said you were going to work here. What's he going to do without you?' Alina felt confused.

'Precisely—he'll be lost, I'm afraid. But you see, I took such a liking to this place, and I knew he'd need someone, so I asked if I could have the job. It's not permanent. He'll get someone else when—when we get—when I get fed up.'

Alina guessed she had been going to say 'when we get married'. She wondered what had made her change her mind. 'Won't you miss him—when he's away looking after his other interests?'

'Like hell!' laughed Vanessa. 'But think how much fun we'll have catching up. Besides, knowing Lucas, he's quite likely to drop in at any time. And when I say drop in I mean that literally. He has a helicopter, you know, and he's a devil for taking people by surprise.'

Surprise being the operative word, thought Alina. They were coming thickly, one after the other. His own helicopter! That took some swallowing. 'You'll be telling me next that he has a boat as well.'

Vanessa grinned. 'He has—a thirty-two-foot yacht. He's just taken me on a two-week cruise round the Greek islands—it was fabulous! You ought to get him to take you when you're better. It'll do you the world of good.'

If you knew how I felt about him you wouldn't suggest that, thought Alina. You'd try your hardest to keep us apart. 'I don't somehow think he'd agree to it,' she said quietly. 'We haven't that sort of relationship.'

'No.' Vanessa looked solemn for a moment. 'Perhaps it wouldn't be such a good idea after all. Sorry I mentioned it.'

Alina drank her tea and dutifully ate the boiled egg, then Vanessa said, 'I'll run you a warm bath. It will make you feel better, and then perhaps you'll be able to catch up on some sleep.'

It sounded a good idea, but Alina found to her surprise that she could not walk to the bathroom unaided. She had not realised exactly how much her illness had taken out of her.

She did feel better afterwards, though, and as Vanessa had predicted fell asleep almost immediately. When she awoke she was amazed to see Lucas in her room.

His back was towards her as he stared out of the window and for a moment she was able to observe him unnoticed. It was rarely he wore a suit these days. Casual clothes seemed to be the order of the day and this afternoon he was dressed in close-fitting grey slacks and a pale blue sweatshirt which seemed moulded to every curve of his muscular body.

She ached to reach out and touch him, to feel those strong arms about her, and ill or not she could not quite quench a primitive urge to have him make love to her.

Her response to even the sight of him was amazing, and as though aware that her eyes were upon him Lucas slowly turned. He smiled and for once there was no harshness. 'Vanessa told me you'd taken a turn for the worse.'

Alina returned his smile, her lips trembling slightly. He did this to her. 'She's exaggerating—I'm really feeling much better.'

'I must say you don't look too bad,' he said. 'I've been watching you while you slept. You were smiling. Were you having a pleasant dream?'

She shook her head. 'I don't remember.' But it was a lie. She had been dreaming of him. They were on his yacht, far out at sea, with no one but seabirds for company. He had admitted that he had made a mistake in running away, but thought her too young to be tied down, thought she might regret it, and he could not have stood it if she had left him. They had made love on the deck. And then her dream had jumped and they had a child—a son—the image of his father—and Lucas had said, 'All I hope is that when he grows up and marries he finds someone like you. If he does he'll be happy and contented for the rest of his life.'

She guessed it was this compliment that had caused her to smile. In her dream it had made her feel humble and very much loved—and very safe.

'I think you do remember,' he said. 'But don't worry, I won't force you to tell me. Dreams are very private, but they can also have a very profound effect if you happen to believe in them. Do you believe in dreams, Alina?'

'No.' She wished she could. 'They're nonsense, a load of rubbish. Things that you dream about couldn't possibly happen.'

'Because you don't want them to, or because you'd be afraid?' It was almost as though he knew she had dreamt about him!

She shrugged. 'Either way. It depends what you're dreaming. Where's Vanessa?' she changed the subject.

'Busy,' he said abruptly. 'The brochures have arrived. I've already made out a mailing list, and she's typing envelopes. I'm afraid she won't be able to give you so much attention for a while.'

'It doesn't matter,' said Alina. 'I'm feeling better. I can look after myself now.'

He frowned abruptly. 'I think not—not for a few more days at least. I'll make you a drink.' He disappeared into her kitchen and she heard him fill the kettle, whistling while he worked. He returned five minutes later with tea and biscuits—but only one cup! She felt disappointed.

'Aren't you having any?'

'I have to much to do. Now I know you're all right I can get on with it.'

Alina glanced at him sharply. 'Don't tell me you were concerned? I can't believe it.'

'Why shouldn't I be?' His dark brows rose into the thatch of blond hair that hung over his forehead.

'Because—when you found me at the bottom of those steps all you did was shout. You gave me the impression that I was a nuisance. I could have managed perfectly well without you, you know. And you didn't need to give me the services of your precious private and personal assistant.'

A hint of a smile curved his lips. 'So Vanessa's been

telling you a little about herself. You know then that she's going to work here for a while?'

Vanessa's told me more than that, Alina could have said, but she merely inclined her head. 'So I understand. Do you think you'll manage without her? From what I gather she's a very important part of your life.'

The smile deepened. 'She is. She's a wonderful, wonderful person. I can't imagine life without her. But I expect I'll survive—and it won't be for ever.'

But he had been prepared to go without herself for ever! Despair gripped Alina's heart. What had Vanessa got that she hadn't? Alina could hold her own with any woman, she knew that without being big-headed. So why did Lucas prefer this other woman?

She snapped a biscuit in two and popped it into her mouth, but she had to sip her tea to make it go down.

'You look disapproving,' he commented. 'I thought Vanessa would be company for you. Don't you like her?'

'Of course I like her, but I shan't see that much of her when I'm back at work.'

His eyes narrowed. 'You're not jealous? You wouldn't have liked the job yourself?'

'And leave you a free field to take over my shop?' she thrust scornfully. 'You must be joking!'

'You've not accepted me yet, then?' The chiselled planes of his face hardened noticeably. 'You still don't trust me?'

'Will I ever?' She glared defiantly. 'We're poles apart now, you and I. Too much has happened for us to trust or accept one another again.' Inwardly her body was crying out for him. It surprised her that she could be like this. The outer condemning shell that she showed Lucas was not the real Alina. Inside she was as warm and loving as ever she had been, and it was sheer hell trying to keep a strict rein on her emotions. Anger was her only defence.

'So far as I'm concerned, you and Vanessa don't exist. Once I'm better I shall go about my daily work and ignore all that's happening to my home. It's something I must reluctantly put up with, but can do nothing about.'

His face was murderous all of a sudden. 'You uncaring little bitch! I just happen to be doing you one big favour. Who the hell do you think you are, talking to me like that? If I hadn't felt sorry for you in the first place I'd never have——'

Alina cut him off furiously. 'I didn't ask for your pity. All I wanted was money—and I don't reckon you're doing me much of a favour in that direction either. But if you're having second thoughts then let's forget the whole thing.' Two spots of colour flared in the paleness of her face, her eyes were bright and angry and she wished she had the strength to get out of bed and hit him.

'It's a bit late for that,' he snarled. 'Why did you sign the damn contract if you weren't sure what you were doing?'

'Don't I wish I hadn't,' she retorted. 'You and your smooth talk! I need my head examining!'

'Or your backside spanking,' he growled. 'You're behaving like a spoilt child. Hell, Alina, you're an adult now, living in a harsh, adult world. You can't shut your eyes to something simply because you don't agree with it.'

'But I can have a damn good try!' she yelled. 'Seeing Wythenhall Manor taken over like this by complete strangers is breaking my heart—don't you understand that? Or have you become so callous that you don't think people should have feelings any more?'

For a brief moment he stood perfectly still. 'I'm not a stranger.'

There was something in his tone that told her she had gone far enough, but Alina was past caring. 'No? You could have fooled me. You're certainly not the same man I once knew—and loved! He was gentle and caring and kind—and wouldn't hurt a fly. You couldn't care less who you tread underfoot so long as you make money out of it in the end!'

'And is that your considered opinion of me?'

Alina swallowed and nodded, her eyes on her cup.

'Look at me, damn you!'

There was a belligerent expression on her face as she obeyed.

Lucas cursed and lunged at her, knocking her cup flying, a brown stain immediately spreading on the cream satin bedcover. His hard hands pinned her shoulders back against the pillows, and the face that loomed over her was a dark angry red.

'Get off or I'll scream,' she threatened, feeling her palms grow moist, knowing that she was entirely at his mercy, that she hadn't the strength to push him away.

'No one will hear you,' he jeered. 'Scream all you like, we're too far away to be overheard.'

'So what are you going to do?' she demanded. 'Strangle me? A slow painful death, is that what you're thinking? Do you hate me that much?'

'Oh, no.' His eyes were alight with malicious amusement. 'That would be far too easy a way out. I have something much more devious in mind.'

His mouth closed on hers before she could say another word, and despite her antagonism Alina felt an unwitting response being drawn from her.

She heard his groan of satisfaction as he parted her lips, plundering the soft moistness, and she wondered for how long she could keep her control.

His kisses were all and more than she remembered, and although with a struggle she maintained a show of indifference, inside she was burning up. Desire was swelling like a flood and she knew that if she did not stop him her river of emotion would burst its banks.

Rigidly she kept her arms at her sides beneath the sheets, her fingers cutting into her palms. Her head lay perfectly still where it was pressed against the pillow, her eyes remained tightly closed. She did not want to see him, she did not want to look into his dearly loved face—because if she did all would be lost.

It took a few minutes for Lucas to realise that he was not getting anywhere, then he pushed himself away abruptly. 'Dammit, Alina, you've changed. You're one hell of a hard woman.'

And you did it to me, she thought bitterly, looking at last into the angry depths of his eyes.

'But I've not finished with you yet.'

'What's that supposed to mean?' she snapped. 'If you're thinking of trying again I shouldn't bother, you'll be doomed to disappointment. I'm immune to you now.'

'We'll see about that.' His breathing was ragged, his chest heaving beneath the cotton shirt.

Alina felt a thrill of excitement as she looked at the naked passion revealed on his face. 'It will take a better man than you to get through to me,' she returned bravely. 'Caveman tactics leave me stone cold.'

His eyes gleamed. 'You prefer the gentle touch? I'll bear that in mind—for next time.'

'There won't be a next time,' she thrust. 'I'm getting up out of this bed—and, I hope, out of your life. I've had as much of you as I can take!'

'That's a pity,' he sneered coldly, 'because I have no intention of leaving here just yet. I shall be around for quite some time and there'll simply be no way of avoiding me.'

'Won't there?' Alina tossed her head proudly. 'We'll have to see about that! Just as you put the rest of the house out of bounds to me, this flat is out of bounds to you. Set foot in it again and I shall be forced to take legal action!'

The ice-cold hardness in her voice seemed to get through to him at last. Savagely he swung on his heel and left the room. Even before the door closed Alina burst into tears.

CHAPTER SIX

IT was a long time before Alina stopped crying. She could not understand what Lucas was trying to do to her. It seemed as though he had taken it as a personal affront because she no longer responded to him—if he only knew! Perhaps his male ego had been damaged? Perhaps he was not accustomed to women spurning him? Or was it a matter of honour that he make her succumb again to his undisputed charm? And then what? Heartbreak all over again? No, thank you very much, she had had enough of that to last her a lifetime. And the only way to stop herself from responding was to avoid seeing him—if that were possible!

With an effort Alina managed to drag herself to the bathroom and was horrified to see the effects of her tears. Her eyes were red and swollen, her cheeks blotchy. She looked a sight?

She splashed her face with cold water, holding a flannel over her eyes, and after a while began to look better. She brushed her hair and applied a little make-up to camouflage the rest of the damages, and had just returned to bed when Vanessa appeared.

'My,' she said, 'there's no need to ask how you're feeling! Make-up now, eh? Do you want to get up for a while? I've just laid the table for me and Lucas, I can easily set an extra place.'

'No,' said Alina quickly. Too quickly, perhaps, for Vanessa shot her a puzzled glance. 'I'll have mine on a tray—if you have time? Lucas did say you were busy.'

'Not too busy to look after you,' Vanessa smiled.

'And I really am pleased to see you looking so much better. I was quite worried this morning.'

Alina nodded. 'Lucas said.'

'Oh, he's been to see you?' Vanessa smiled knowingly. 'Does that account for the colour in your cheeks? He's been cheering you up, has he?'

'Like a wet Monday.' Alina could not hold back her bitterness.

Vanessa's fine brows rose. 'You've not been arguing again?'

Alina shrugged. 'Do we ever do anything else? I wish he'd never come back, I really do. Can't you use your influence, Vanessa, and get him away for a while?'

'In the middle of a new project?' Vanessa looked surprised. 'You don't know him very well. He won't move out of here until this thing's got going. He might nip off for the odd day, but that will be all. Sorry, Alina, but you're stuck with him. Why don't you kiss and make up?'

Swift colour flooded Alina's cheeks. Vanessa could not have got nearer to the truth if she had tried. 'Too much water's passed under the bridge. We barely tolerate each other. I'm beginning to wish I hadn't let him help me—in fact I told him so.'

Vanessa pulled a wry face. 'And I guess he didn't take too kindly to that?'

'He said it was too late for second thoughts. I can't understand how you stick him, Vanessa. He's impossible.' But she could really. Vanessa loved him—and what was more important, he loved her!

'We understand each other,' said Vanessa simply. 'I'll fetch your tray up.'

The next day Alina was already out of bed and dressed when Vanessa came in with her breakfast. She felt dreadfully weak and it had taken an age to drag on her clothes, but she had made it, and now faced the copper-haired girl with a smile.

'I'm better, isn't that marvellous? I shan't need your services any longer. You can devote yourself to your boss.' And you're welcome, she added under her breath.

Vanessa looked sceptical. 'You don't get over 'flu that quickly. I bet you can hardly stand, if the truth's known. But if it's Lucas you're afraid of, he's gone to London for the day. Something urgent cropped up.'

Alina's smile widened. 'That's the best piece of news I've heard in a long time. I want to look over the house, see what's been going on while I've been ill. Will you take me on a guided tour?'

'If you think you're up to it?' Vanessa grinned conspiratorially.

'On my knees if necessary,' laughed Alina. She had never thought it possible she could be friends with a girl who was going to marry Lucas, but Vanessa was so cheerful and helpful, never complaining no matter what she was asked to do, it was impossible to dislike her.

And as Lucas had made it clear that he no longer had any interest in her, Alina, there was not much she could do except accept the situation and push her own feelings to the back of her mind.

The two girls munched their way through scrambled eggs and toast and drank a pot of tea, then Alina announced that she was ready.

Vanessa gave her her arm and led the way to the bedrooms on the first floor. Alina had already seen those upstairs and she doubted whether she would have the energy to make it up there anyway.

She was impressed—there was no doubt about it. Each room had a different colour scheme, echoed throughout the wallpaper, carpets and bedlinen, even to matching colours for the towels in the bathrooms.

'All this trouble for businessmen!' she laughed. 'It will be lost on them.'

'There'll be women too,' said Vanessa, 'and they'll appreciate it. I can't get over the fact that you once lived in this part of the house. All these rooms! They're magnificent. Did your mother entertain a lot?'

Alina nodded. 'And in her last years she lived beyond her means. Didn't Lucas tell you that?'

Vanessa shook her head. 'He merely said you had financial problems. Exactly what or how or why he didn't go into.'

This surprised Alina. She had assumed that Lucas had discussed everything with his red-headed girl-friend. 'Oh, yes. It came as quite a shock to discover that they'd left enormous debts behind. I suppose really the sensible thing would have been to sell, but when you've lived your whole life in a place, especially somewhere like this, it becomes sort of part of you. I could never imagine living anywhere else.'

'It would certainly be a come-down,' agreed Vanessa. 'I can see that now. But turning it into this conference centre was really a superb idea. It's lost nothing, has it? In fact it's been given a face-lift.'

They had by now reached what was going to be the second of the meeting rooms. An enormous room with an arched, oak-beamed ceiling and a polished oak floor, with an immense open fireplace at one end, and a gallery at the other.

It had been fitted out with projectors and screens and different sorts of lighting and rows of chairs, and it all looked very impressive. Yet at the same time none of the original décor had been spoiled. Everything could be whipped out and no one would be any the wiser. It could again be turned into a family home if it was wanted.

Downstairs, the other big room had had nothing more done to it than a coat of paint. The big table was ideal for meetings, and there were the easy chairs for anything less formal. The only addition was a bar in the corner.

The room which had been the family's sitting room-cum-dining room, and what had been termed the inner hall when the house was first built, had now been made into a reception area, housing nothing more than a long counter and chairs and loads of pot plants lit by strategically placed lighting.

At the other side of yet another huge stone fireplace was a door which led into a small room which had been used by Alina's family to store junk.

'I don't believe it,' laughed Alina, when Vanessa proudly took her inside, announcing that this was her new office. 'It used to be full of empty boxes and my old rocking horse and a sewing machine and—oh, whole loads of stuff. I never knew it was so big.'

Indeed, cleaned out and redecorated, with a carpet on the floor, it was a very passable office. There was a desk near the window and a filing cabinet and a telephone. There was a washbasin and a kettle and some cups and saucers.

'I see you intend looking after yourself.' Alina flopped down on to the chair near the desk. 'Actually I could do with a cup of tea now. How about it?'

'Me, too,' agreed Vanessa, filling the kettle. 'You've not overdone it? You look quite pale.'

'To tell you the truth,' admitted Alina. 'I'm not so strong as I thought I was. I'm sure someone's stuffed my legs with cotton wool!'

The telephone rang suddenly, startling them both. Vanessa paused in the act of popping tea-bags into the pot. 'Perhaps it's an enquiry. Wouldn't it be fun if we booked something before Lucas comes back? You answer it, Alina.'

'But I'm not supposed to have anything to do with the handling of this, you know. Lucas's orders,' returned Alina primly, trying to stop herself smiling. Vanessa really was great company.

'Well, I say you can,' laughed Vanessa. 'Find out who it is and when I've made the tea I'll take over.'

Alina picked up the brand new brilliant red telephone, with its brand new telephone number. 'Wythenhall Manor Conference Centre,' she said in her best voice. 'Can I help you?'

'Vanessa darling, a quick word. I'm afraid I won't be able to get back tonight after all. Things are in a stinking mess, and I have to sort them out. Oh, hell,' his voice dropped to a low sexy growl, 'I wish you were here, I really do.'

Alina's heart stopped beating. She wanted to tell him that he had made a mistake, explain that it wasn't his darling Vanessa he was speaking to, but somehow she couldn't. The words stuck in her throat and all she could do was hold on to the telephone and listen in fascinated horror, while a prickly heat warmed her skin.

'No one else in the world can match up to you, Vanessa. And if you insist on staying there for the whole summer God knows what I'm going to do without you. You're my right arm, don't you know that? Without you I'm lost.'

Alina gave a choking cough and passed the phone to Vanessa, who by this time had made the tea. 'What is it?' she mouthed, seeing Alina's ashen face, 'an obscene phone call?'

You could say that, thought Alina. Lucas whispering sweet nothings to his mistress was obscene.

'Hello,' said Vanessa crisply. 'Who is this? Oh, it's you, Lucas. What on earth have you been saying to Alina? She's as white as a sheet!'

Alina closed her eyes, trying to control her ragged breathing, but hearing only Lucas's deeply sensual voice reverberating in her head. *Darling!* The word was a caress. *Without you I'm lost.* A cry from the heart.

And then Vanessa was laughing. 'Oh, Lucas, you shouldn't say that, not now. There's a time and place for everything, didn't you know?' But she looked happy and there was a delicate flush to her cheeks.

She sat on the edge of the desk, swinging her leg, listening attentively, agreeing with whatever it was he was saying. 'You're a slave-driver,' she laughed, 'but I love you, and you don't have to beg because you know I'll do it—just because it's you.'

They spoke for a few minutes more, during which time Alina was able to pull herself together sufficiently to pretend that nothing was wrong.

'That man has superhuman energy,' grumbled Vanessa when she put down the phone, 'and he thinks everyone else is the same.' But she was smiling. 'I've got to dash into Cheltenham and meet the London train. He's sent me some work, would you believe? Some new project he's presenting and he reckons no one else can type it out as neatly or as accurately as me. I have a sneaking suspicion it's because he thinks I'm going to sit around here doing nothing. Can I borrow your car?'

Alina nodded, her head spinning at this sudden whirlwind of activity.

'Oh, and Lucas said he can't think what he said to upset you. But he apologises and says why didn't you say who you were.'

'Or did he ask what I was doing in your office?' asked Alina acidly.

'Is that what you were afraid of?' Vanessa's beautiful green eyes widened. 'I see. He really has got to you, hasn't he? I can't think why, considering you were once such good friends.'

'Once, being the operative word,' said Alina. 'Have you got time for your tea or do you have to go running when the big white chief snaps his fingers?'

Vanessa smiled and looked at the new clock on the wall. 'I can manage ten minutes. The train's not due for another half hour.'

Afterwards, when Vanessa had gone, Alina renewed her explorations. Her mother's kitchen had always been filled with the latest labour-saving devices, but now it was even more impressive with a brand new electric range where cooking for large numbers would be no problem. And loads of new china and glassware and cutlery had arrived, all stacked neatly in a cupboard situated between the kitchen and the dining room, together with tablecloths and napkins.

The dining room had once been a lounge. Now all the comfortable chairs had been transferred to the meeting room and in their place was a series of small tables and chairs. They were of a very high quality, and Alina could not fault Lucas's taste.

When she finally returned to her own quarters she was exhausted and for the rest of the day did nothing but sit around, seeing nothing more of Vanessa, and going to bed early.

Having so much time on her hands, though, it was very difficult not to think about Lucas, and his words of endearment to Vanessa did nothing but fill her mind. What had merely been supposition had now been driven home as hard fact, and she knew that the sooner she got back to the shop the better.

Over the next few days her strength gradually returned, until she felt at last that she was fit enough to take up the reins again. Lucas had still not come back, and she had seen so little of Vanessa that she might not have been there.

On the rare occasions when she did venture into the other part of the house she heard the typewriter being pounded, and the girl had her sympathies. Lucas was a hard taskmaster. He would not suit her, she knew, but strangely Vanessa seemed to revel in it. She would do anything for Lucas, she had said on the phone, and this proved it. She worked from morning till night, with only short breaks for refreshments—and seemed to be enjoying it! Perhaps it was Lucas's appreciation at the end of the day which was her reward!

The thought was a bitter pill to swallow, and Alina wished she had never allowed herself to become involved with Lucas again.

The morning that Alina did go back to work she felt as though she was walking into a different shop. It had changed—drastically. One wall had been knocked down to incorporate what had been empty premises next door. There was very little left of her old stock, instead there were some very beautiful pieces of furniture—including the Georgian writing table and the gold chaise-lounge which she had been outbid against at one of the sales!

So—maybe Lucas had been innocent of spreading those ugly rumours, but he had certainly not been so blameless in stopping her from buying. It made her glad that she had not yet apologised. He did not deserve it.

But what she could not understand was why he had gone to this trouble now—unless it was still in his mind that he would take this over as well. He surely couldn't have done it for her sake alone?

Alina had been there for no more than a minute or two when a very smart, attractive woman in her mid-fifties arrived, stalking in as though she owned the place. She looked at Alina in surprise. 'How did you get in?'

'What do you mean, how did I get in?' asked Alina sharply. 'This is my shop, that's how.' It took her no more than a few seconds to guess that this was the person Lucas had employed to look after it in her absence.

'Oh,' said the woman, looking slightly deflated. 'I had no idea you were coming back yet. Lucas never said.' She held out her hand. 'My name's Penny Marshall.'

She had deep auburn hair, short and thick, waving slightly about her attractive face. She wore a knitted suit in palest cream, and a string of pearls about her neck.

Alina took her hand, 'Alina Stewart,' and wondered whether Lucas had a penchant for redheaded women. The thought made her smile, and because Penny Marshall looked slightly uncomfortable she said, 'Never mind, I'm not quite up to it yet. I shall be glad of your help for a day or two.' And then she wondered why she had said that because really she resented Lucas planting this woman here without consulting her. 'I thought I'd walked into the wrong place,' she continued. 'How did he get this done so quickly, and why?'

Penny smiled wryly. 'Lucas is a doer. Everything has to be done yesterday so far as he's concerned. He's a wonderful man to work for, though. Don't you think it's an improvement?'

Alina shrugged. 'I don't think trade warrants it. I don't suppose he thought of the fact that my overheads will go up?' And that would mean less money out of which to pay her rent!

'It's been doing pretty well,' said Penny. 'I run one of his shops in London and actually I was quite surprised. When he asked me to come here I thought I'd be in for a quiet time. In fact I've been really busy.'

Alina could not understand this. In her experience trade in this shop was never brisk.

As the day progressed she discovered that she and Penny, who was a widow, had many things in common and they got on well. The fact that the woman was old enough to be her mother did not seem to enter into it. Penny was young for her age, dressed well, and had modern ideas. By the end of the day Alina had invited her back for a meal.

'Heavens, if I'd known you were at the Coach House by yourself all this time I'd have made sure you got invited before. I'm surprised at Lucas.'

Penny smiled mysteriously. 'He did ask, but Lucas has Vanessa.'

Those three words said it all, thought Alina dismally, not realising her lips had compressed and a bleakness filled her eyes.

'You've not fallen for Lucas yourself?' laughed the older woman. 'It happens to everyone, but they get over it when they discover he's not the settling-down type. Rumour has it that he was let down badly at one stage in his life and now won't let himself trust any woman. Except Vanessa, of course. But theirs is a very special relationship, as I expect you've noticed?'

Alina tried to join in Penny's laughter. 'I've known Lucas since I was about six. He's no more than a big brother to me.' But who was she trying to kid? Penny or herself? And who was this woman who had let him down? Another part of his life that she knew nothing about?

It turned out to be quite a party that evening. When they arrived back at Wythenhall Manor Lucas's distinctive silver car was outside, as well as another two which Alina had not seen before.

She heard the sound of male voices as she took Penny up to her flat, but preferred not to stay and find out to whom they belonged. No doubt she would discover their identity soon enough.

Alina had done nothing more than settle Penny with a magazine and a cup of tea when Vanessa burst in. 'You're eating with us tonight,' she began. 'Lucas has—oh, hello, Mrs Marshall, I didn't know you were here. Good, you can join us. It will even up the numbers.'

The older woman said, 'Hello, Vanessa, and please call me Penny, but it's up to Alina whether we come. She's kindly invited me to eat with her.'

Vanessa smiled confidently. 'Oh, she'll come. By the way, how did your first day go? Are you absolutely shattered?'

'Not too bad, with Penny's help,' she said. 'And I suppose I have no choice about the meal if Lucas has arranged it. Was it an invitation or a command?'

Understanding her perfectly, Vanessa said, 'It's a get-together dinner. The new manager's here, and the cook, and Lucas wants us all to get to know one another.'

'And where do I fit in?' asked Alina, suddenly scathing. 'Is he forgetting that I have no part in all this?'

Penny Marshall looked at her in bewilderment, evidently wondering what all this double-talk was about. Vanessa rested a comforting arm on Alina's shoulder. 'There you go again, misjudging Lucas! He's not that bad.'

Because you're biased, thought Alina, though she

smiled wanly. 'Maybe. But because Penny's here, and because I think she deserves some entertainment after being on her own at the Coach House for so long we'll come.'

Penny raised her hands in horror. 'If you're against the idea as much as you seem to be, don't do it for my benefit. The two of us here suits me fine.'

Vanessa grinned and skipped to the door. 'See you later, folks. About seven, he said. Don't keep him waiting.'

'Like a brother, eh?' queried Penny when she had gone. 'There doesn't sound much brotherly affection there. Would you think it awfully rude if I asked what was wrong?'

Alina sighed and sat down, tucking her legs beneath her. No way was she going to tell this woman the whole truth, but she supposed she owed her some explanation. It could be an explosive evening and it was only right that Penny should understand a little of the situation.

'You know this place was once my home?'

Penny nodded. 'And now you're in partnership with Lucas, turning it into this splendid business centre. So where's the problem?'

'The problem is Lucas,' said Alina, her lips twisting wryly, her eyes wide and apologetic. 'The partnership is on paper only, in reality he has taken over.'

'And you resent it?' Penny nodded understandably. 'But Lucas is that type of man. When he does something he puts his heart and soul into it and he takes charge. Surely you know that?'

'I'm beginning to,' admitted Alina. 'I haven't seen him for eight years. You wouldn't believe how he's changed. I find it difficult to accept.'

'We all change,' said Penny. 'I expect he sees a difference in you. But why let it ruin your life? If he

wants to do all the donkey work, so be it. You'll get
your fair share of the rewards. Besides, you have your
shop, isn't that enough?'

'That's what he says.' Alina wondered why no one
else could see her point of view. 'But even there he
couldn't resist putting his oar in.'

'It's an improvement, so be thankful,' smiled
Penny. 'He must have your interests at heart or he
wouldn't bother.'

Or he wanted to ruin her altogether! But she kept
her thoughts to herself. It was obvious this woman
was on Lucas's side. Alina would say this for him, his
staff were devoted and loyal. He must have some
virtues, even if she had yet to discover them.

'I suppose we'd better get ready,' she said, glancing
at her watch. 'His lordship won't like it if we're late.
Do you want me to nip you over to the Coach House
for a change of clothes?'

'Heavens, no!' said Penny. 'I'll do as I am. I'm too
old to want to impress.'

Or perhaps it was because she knew that she looked
exactly right? Like Vanessa, the woman had impec-
cable taste. Lucas certainly knew how to pick them.
Perhaps he liked surrounding himself with beautiful
women? It made her wonder how many others there
were, and it made her almost decide to dress in old
jeans and a sweater with her hair scraped back
unbecomingly and her face bare of make-up.

But somehow she did not think she would quite
have the nerve to carry it off. Had she been dining
with Lucas alone, she would have done, but there
were the others to consider. She was Lucas's business
partner and must act accordingly, even if only for the
benefit of the two unknown men.

An hour later she was ready, dressed in a smart
oatmeal-coloured suit, with a tan frilled blouse and tan

high-heeled sandals which made her legs look slimmer
and longer than usual. She had brushed her hair until
it shone and left it loose about her face and shoulders.

'How do I look?' she asked Penny.

Carefully shaped brows rose. 'Dressed for the kill, I
would suspect, if I didn't know better. But if you're
after a boost for your morale you've certainly got it.
You look feminine, yet—lethal, dare I say? A business
woman with a hint of a very sexy lady underneath.
Mind you don't have Vanessa after your blood!'

Alina laughed. 'Vanessa and I understand each
other.'

'Then you've no problems,' said Penny. 'Let's go
and see what other interesting men are on the menu
tonight.'

They found them in the big room where the bar had
been installed, sitting in comfortable armchairs, drinks
in front of them, a huge log fire toasting their toes. At
the other end the table was set in readiness for their
meal.

As they approached Lucas jumped up, followed
more slowly by the other two men. He acknowledged
Penny briefly, then turned his attention to Alina, his
eyes drifting over her with a slow sensuous appraisal.

She felt her colour rise and said defiantly, 'Well,
aren't you going to introduce us? Isn't that supposed
to be the whole idea of this evening?'

He smiled grimly. 'Do forgive me. You look so
stunning I almost forgot myself.'

Alina saw Penny's satisfied smile and suddenly felt
very much in command. 'Thank you,' she said
demurely, and looked expectantly at the other two
men.

The one in shirt sleeves she guessed was the cook,
the other in a quiet grey lounge suit was looking at her
as though he could not quite believe that she was real.

'Bruce Holden,' said Lucas, following her line of vision. 'He's going to manage this place. You'll probably see quite a lot of him. Bruce, this is Alina Stewart.'

Bruce had an engaging grin and a shock of sandy-brown hair and the hand which shook Alina's was firm. 'I've heard a lot about you,' he said. The voice matched the face, warm and friendly, and he seemed to have difficulty in taking his eyes off her.

'In that case I hope it was good,' she smiled back, 'and I also hope that you'll be happy working here.'

'I'm sure I shall be,' he returned, and he had no need to say that she was behind his reasoning.

'And this is Danny Rafferty,' said Lucas sharply, as much to say that she had spent quite enough time holding Bruce's hand. 'He's taking charge in the kitchen.'

She switched her smile to Danny, again getting the feeling that he was impressed, and she was glad she had taken care over her appearance.

'Mr Delgado is fortunate to have such a beautiful partner,' said Danny. 'It will be my pleasure to work for you both.'

Alina glanced at Penny, who now sat quietly talking to Vanessa. They both smiled encouragingly and Vanessa stuck up her thumb, as though to say, you're doing well there, girl, keep it up!

Lucas was the only one who was not smiling. He looked out of sorts and said brusquely, 'What would you like to drink, Alina?'

She looked at him from beneath her thick lashes. 'Have you forgotten I don't drink?'

His angry shrug suggested that he had. 'An orange juice, then, or tonic water?'

'Orange will do fine,' she said demurely, and turned her attention to Bruce. 'Are you familiar with this part of the country?'

He took her elbow and led her to a seat, perching himself on the arm. 'I'm a Londoner, actually, but I'm sure I shall like it here. The scenery is—er— particularly exciting.'

His eyes were on her as he spoke and Alina lapped up his flattery, smiling warmly, and hardly looking at Lucas when he handed her her glass.

It had been a long time since she felt so at ease with any man, and if this was one method of arming herself against Lucas, then she intended to take it.

Danny disappeared, returning a short time later to announce that dinner was ready. Alina found herself sitting opposite Lucas, who was between the other two women. Bruce was on her one side and presumably Danny would take up the other as soon as he had served their meal.

Bruce immediately devoted the whole of his attention to her. 'Lucas told me a little about your predicament. I think it's very courageous of you to start this new venture. Most women I know would have sold up and considered themselves lucky. Wythenhall Manor must mean a great deal to you. Has it been in the family long?'

'No,' smiled Alina warmly. 'My parents bought it shortly after they got married.' She wondered exactly how much Lucas had told this man. 'But it sort of grows on you. I had intended remaining here after I married myself, and then handing it down to my own children.'

'And now you've had to do this. Poor you!' He sounded genuinely concerned. 'Perhaps one day you'll be rich enough to restore it back into a family home.'

'It's what I would like,' admitted Alina, 'except that now Lucas has half shares. It will never be mine again.'

'You can always buy him out—when you've made your pile.'

Or marry him, thought Alina bitterly, that would be the ideal solution. She glanced across. He was talking to Vanessa. Whatever he was saying looked urgent, and when he had finished Vanessa leaned towards him and kissed his cheek. He turned so that their lips met and Alina felt jealous pain stab through her like a knife.

She caught Penny's eyes on her, thoughtful, concerned, and realised that his older woman knew exactly what she was thinking. She attempted a vague smile and turned once again to Bruce. 'Do you really think it will be all that successful?'

'If I have anything to do with it, it will be,' he said positively. 'I found the challenge stimulating before I met you. Now I'm even more determined that Wythenhall Manor will be *the* place that all the top companies will want for their conventions.'

Alina found his enthusiasm infectious, and her eyes brightened. 'You know something, Bruce, I think I believe you. With you and Lucas working for the same end it can't fail.'

'But whereas Lucas will be doing it for what he can get out of it, I shall be doing it for you.' He picked up her hand and raised it gallantly to his lips. 'You're a very beautiful, desirable woman, Alina. I certainly hope we shall see a lot more of each other.'

Alina was unaware that Lucas had been listening. Now his harsh voice bit into their conversation. 'I shouldn't count on seeing her too often, Holden. You will have your work and Miss Stewart has hers. Also, I forbid it. I can see your job suffering as the result of such a dalliance, and if you feel I'm imposing too harsh a restriction then I suggest you hand in your notice right now and I'll find someone to replace you.'

CHAPTER SEVEN

A DEATHLY silence followed Lucas's words. All eyes were upon first him and then Bruce. Alina could not believe she had heard him correctly.

Bruce looked shocked and hurt and Alina fully expected him to storm out. But he didn't. He looked at Lucas stonily, lips compressed. 'You're the boss, but you have no say over what I do in my spare time.'

'What spare time?' snapped Lucas. 'You agreed when you took this job that you'd work all the hours that God made—and those were your own words. Is your memory so short?'

Alina was aware of Bruce's tension and felt sorry for him. She did not feel that Lucas was treating him fairly. 'You're being unreasonable, Lucas.'

'I'm merely reminding Mr Holden of our agreement,' he said sharply. 'And I'm sure he doesn't need you to stick up for him.'

Bruce smiled at her before looking back across the table. 'I'm well aware of what I said.'

'But you didn't know you would meet someone as attractive as Miss Stewart, is that it?'

Looking momentarily nonplussed, Bruce said, 'I intend doing my job to the best of my ability, Mr Delgado. I can say no more than that.'

Lucas nodded curtly. 'Then see that you do,' and his hard eyes rested on Alina for several long seconds before he turned his attention yet again to Vanessa.

Alina glanced at Penny, gave an almost indiscernible shrug and received a warmly sympathetic smile. Bruce seemed disinclined to talk now and she got on with her chicken consommé garnished with diced tomatoes, which Danny had announced as Consommé Cléopâtre.

If this was a taste of his cooking the delegates who came here would certainly want to come again, if only to sample his excellent food.

It was followed by braised gammon in a sherry sauce, served with peaches, and accompanied by buttered whole potatoes and green beans.

Alina congratulated Danny and said to Penny, 'This certainly beats the liver and onions you would have had from me,' and to Bruce, 'Aren't you enjoying this? Isn't Danny an absolute marvel?'

'He's an excellent cook,' agreed Bruce, 'but that's only to be expected. Mr Delgado always demands perfection.' There was no rancour in his voice, merely resigned acceptance.

'You've known him some time?'

'I worked for a company he had a lot to do with, but I wasn't directly employed by him.'

'So this is your first taste of what he's like as a boss?'

Unexpectedly he grinned. 'But to give him his due, he's right. I did say I wouldn't mind working long hours. You see, I've recently been divorced and it seemed the best solution.'

'I'm sorry,' said Alina. 'I didn't know. You wanted to make a new start? What a pity he's spoilt it for you already.'

'I'll survive,' he smiled. 'I'm getting expert at that. When Sally left me I felt as if it was the end of the world, now I've discovered that there's still life going on around me—and other women who could, I'm sure, help me get over her.' He looked at her meanfully.

'You know I'll help if I can,' said Alina. 'But with no strings attached. I'm not ready for an involvement.'

Perceptively he said, 'You too are nursing a broken heart? It's funny, I knew the moment I saw you that we had something in common. Perhaps one day we'll share secrets?'

'Perhaps,' agreed Alina, but she knew she could never discuss Lucas with Bruce. Nor with anyone. Her feelings for him were very private.

Meringue filled with raspberry sorbet followed, and after that they took their coffee to the other end of the room, where they again settled in the comfortable armchairs.

Lucas piled more logs on to the fire and it could have been a pleasant evening, decided Alina, except that he kept a discreet eye on her and Bruce, which made the other man edgy and herself resentful.

She wondered why Lucas objected to Bruce being friendly towards her. Perhaps it was because he was a divorcee? Although she couldn't see what difference that should make.

Consequently she paid Bruce more attention than she might otherwise have done, feeling a grim satisfaction when she sensed Lucas's disapproval, knowing that he would not risk another showdown tonight.

He might get Bruce on his own later and give him a ticking off, but she felt sure he would say nothing more in front of the others.

At length Penny declared it was time she returned to the Coach House.

'Why not stay?' ventured Alina. 'We have all these rooms, I'm sure no one will object.'

But Penny was adamant. 'All my stuff's there. I'd really rather go.'

'Then I'll get my car out.'

Lucas said sharply, 'You two women aren't going alone at this time of night. I'll take you, Penny.'

Alina tilted her chin stubbornly. 'It was my idea she came here, it's up to me to get her back.'

And Bruce added, 'I'll go with them, Lucas.'

Penny laughed. 'All this fuss over who takes me! I'll ring for a taxi, then there'll be no argument.'

'Oh, hell!' slammed Lucas. 'What a way to end what's already been an intolerable evening! For God's sake go with them, Bruce. It shouldn't take more than five minutes.' He looked at his watch as he spoke and they all knew, Alina felt sure, that he was timing them.

They went in Bruce's car and on the way back he pulled in to the side of the road, switching off the engine and turning to Alina. 'I really was serious about getting to know you better. Lucas can't control my free time, no matter what he says. Will you come out with me?' His voice was gently persuasive and he looked anxious.

Alina saw no reason why she should not. It had been a long time since she had dated any other man. Lucas was the only one she had ever desired, everyone else paled in comparison.

She smiled warmly. 'Yes, Bruce, I'd like that.' He was charming and easy to get on with, and so long as he did not expect too much theirs could be a very good relationship.

He leaned across and pecked her cheek. 'Thanks, Alina. You don't know how much this means to me.'

But she thought she did. They had both suffered traumatically. They were kindred souls, and if they could help each other then that was all to the good.

'Tomorrow night?' he pressed. 'Until we're open properly I'm sure I won't be that busy.'

'Tomorrow,' agreed Alina.

'We'll find a nice quiet place for a meal, and we'll talk, and we'll find out all about each other, and——'

As he paused Alina laughed. 'And I think we ought to get back.'

There was no one about when they eventually returned, which surprised her. She had thought Lucas would be hovering somewhere, checking how long it had taken them, ready to have another go at Bruce. Perhaps Vanessa had successfully taken his mind off them? Alina did not know whether to be glad or sorry.

They parted at the door to her flat, Bruce holding her hand for a moment and looking as though he wanted to kiss her, then changing his mind and carrying on up to his room at the top of the house. She closed the door behind her and snapped on the light, moving through into the kitchen.

Lucas's voice over her shoulder came as a distinct shock and she whirled, eyes flashing. 'What the hell are you doing in here? You frightened me to death! Must I lock my apartment in future?'

'I merely wanted to reassure myself that you got back safely,' he said coolly.

'Unmolested, you mean?' she flashed. 'Bruce isn't like that. You should know, you picked him.'

'I also know that it's been a long time since he had a woman. Twelve months he's been divorced and he's looked at no one since.'

'And because he seems to have taken a liking to me, you think it's tantamount to rape?' Alina could not understand why Lucas was acting so peculiarly.

'Now you're being ridiculous,' he snapped. 'You know full well what I mean.'

'No, I don't,' said Alina. 'Suppose you tell me? Exactly what is it that you're afraid of?'

Savagely Lucas swung away, lighting a cigar and drawing on it fiercely. 'He's not good enough for you.'

Alina faced him angrily. 'And what's that supposed to mean? What sort of a man would you suggest I go out with? Someone like yourself, tough and aggressive, who won't stand any nonsense?' This was a pointless conversation, she couldn't see what he was getting at.

'Certainly not a man who's been married,' he said tightly.

She shook her head. 'I can't see what difference it makes. Or are you suggesting that I find myself someone less experienced? You think he might take advantage? You reckon he knows more about women than I know about men? You're right there—he does. But so do you. So what right does that give you to set yourself up as my keeper?'

'You have no one else,' he barked, controlling his temper with great difficulty.

'I'm twenty-four,' she spat, 'completely capable of looking after myself. What I choose to do is none of your business, so I'd be obliged if you'd keep your nose out of it! And——' she paused to give her words maximum effect, 'just for the record, I'm going out with Bruce tomorrow night—and there's nothing you can do about it!'

His face grew grim. 'You're heading for trouble, Alina. Give Bruce an inch and he'll take a mile. It will be all or nothing with him. I can't see him settling for a platonic friendship.'

'Who said that's what I want?' She glared defiantly. 'I've buried myself in my work long enough. It's about time I had some enjoyment!'

She thought he was going to hit her and flinched at the ice-cold hardness in his eyes.

'I won't let any other man have you!' Lucas ground out his cigar with swift impatient movements, gripping her shoulders cruelly, searching her face.

Alina thrilled at his touch. If only it was jealously that motivated him! If only he wanted her, instead of this strange reasoning that she could not understand.

'For Pete's sake, Bruce isn't going to have me, as you so crudely put it,' she cried. 'We're going out for a meal, that's all.'

She felt herself trembling, and so that he should not see the effect he still had on her she lashed out at him, pummelling her fists against his chest. 'Let me go, you swine! Get out! I hate you!'

The rock hardness of his muscles was like a brick wall, her blows having no result whatsoever, except to make him more angry than before. 'You little spitfire!' he thundered, shaking her so violently that her teeth rattled. 'One day you'll thank me for what I'm doing!'

'Like hell I will!' she cried, sinking her teeth into his arm so that he yelled out and abruptly let her go.

'You bitch!' he bellowed. 'I ought to bite you back!'

'Then why don't you?' Defiantly she glared at him.

'Why don't I indeed?' Lucas advanced threateningly, and it took every ounce of Alina's willpower not to step back.

Bravely she held his gaze, and even when he grabbed a handful of hair, forcing back her head so that she could see the dark intention on his face, she did not cry out.

Instead she almost welcomed the pain that he was inflicting. At least it meant that he was taking some notice of her! With a sort of fascinated horror she watched as his mouth closed on her throat, feeling a desperate urge to run her fingers through the thick silver hair that was brushing her face. But his teeth did not break the soft flesh.

With an anguished groan he gathered her to him, seeking her lips instead, kissing her as though his life depended on it. Excitement she could not control consumed Alina, and she returned his kisses with complete abandon, moving her body sensually against his, wishing this moment to go on for ever.

Beneath the thin silk of his shirt she felt his heart pounding and her own raced in response. Without quite knowing what she was doing she undid the buttons and slid her hands inside, exulting in the smooth hardness of his back beneath her fingers.

Her action released his tight control and the next moment he had shrugged out of his shirt completely and was unbuttoning her blouse. More than anything Alina wanted to glory in the close contact of their naked bodies, but she was still sane enough to realise where it could all end.

'No, Lucas! No!' She moved her head away from his demanding lips. 'We mustn't!'

'Why mustn't we?' he growled, pausing for a moment to look at her with passionate intensity. 'You want it as much as I do, and if this is the only way I can make sure Bruce Holden doesn't get you, then so be it.'

Alina felt suddenly sick, hating both herself and Lucas. 'Is that why you're doing it?' And she had thought—It didn't bear thinking about! 'Let me go!'

Lucas laughed, his face twisted with elation and triumph. 'Now we've got this far? Oh, no, my little beauty. You should know by now that I always finish what I start.'

'We've not started anything!' she shrieked. 'You're taking advantage. Let me go or I'll scream and kick and bite—and you'll regret it!'

'It strikes me that you're the one who's doing the regretting,' he sneered.

'Too true I am,' Alina yelled. 'I regret the day my mother ever allowed you to work for us. I wish I'd never set eyes on you!'

'You regret all those good times we had together?' Some of his anger had abated, yet still he held her in an iron-like grip, forcing her against the solid strength of him.

But the physical contact meant nothing to Alina at this moment. She was far too outraged to feel any sexual awareness. 'Every single one of them. The best thing you ever did was to go to London and leave me—and I mean that, Lucas. Don't you ever forget it!'

With a swift intake of breath he thrust her from him so viciously that she fell across the room. 'Something tells me you won't let me forget it. You really know how to hit where it hurts, don't you, Alina?'

'And I suppose you don't?' she hurled, not even attempting to pick herself up. 'But don't try and kid me that you have feelings, because I know better. There's only one person that you care about, and that's yourself. Maybe I ought to warn Vanessa what she's letting herself in for?'

He frowned harshly. 'What's Vanessa got to do with all this, for God's sake?'

'She says you're going to get married.'

The instant shock on his face made Alina wonder whether she had put her foot in it, whether it had been wishful thinking on Vanessa's part.

Her hopes rose valiantly, only to have them dashed the next second when he said, 'Trust Vanessa to let the cat out of the bag.'

'Then it is true?' Alina did not realise how anxious she sounded.

'Would I lie to you?'

Sadly she shook her head. 'Whatever else I might think about you, I don't think you're a liar.'

'At least that's something to be grateful for.' Lucas snatched up his shirt, buttoning it methodically, not once taking his eyes from her face.

'And while I think of it,' she slammed, 'I'd like to tell you that I resent you interfering in my shop. I don't have much choice about what you do here, but that is my domain and I'd thank you to keep your nose out of it!'

His brows rose. 'Penny thought it was a good idea. It's a vast improvement, and I believe trade is on the up.'

'It has nothing to do with Penny,' she snapped. 'Business has improved, but——'

'But you can't stomach the thought that it's because of something I've done?' His lip curled contemptuously. 'Do me a favour, Alina, learn to accept help gracefully.'

'Oh—*you!*' She scrambled to her feet and hurled herself at him, but he quickly let himself out and she heard his harsh laughter echo down the stairs.

Bitterly she leaned against the door. The shop wasn't really that important. What mattered was Lucas's impending marriage. Always she had cherished a hope that Vanessa might be romanticising, that their love might be a one-sided affair and nothing would come of it. But now she had confirmation that one day they would indeed become man and wife!

It was hard, indisputable fact, and there was nothing at all that she could do about it—except learn to live with it. There was no running away, no escaping. She and Lucas were inextricably tied together and she could either accept the situation, or make herself ill by worrying about it.

Not bothering now to make a drink, she dragged herself to bed, stepping out of her clothes and leaving them in a heap on the floor. But sleep would not come. She had not expected it to. Her pillow grew damp with tears as sobs racked her body, and it was several long hours before she eventually grew calmer.

An almost full moon threw patches of light into the room, somewhere an owl hooted and bats screamed—but in the house there was silence!

Alina wondered what Vanessa and Lucas were doing. Had he told her about his scene with Alina? Were they even now making love? It did not bear thinking about. But it was a cold, stark fact that she had to accept.

When dawn sent chill fingers of light stealing across the sky she still had not slept. She ran a hot bath and lay in it for almost an hour, trying to restore some feeling into her numbed body and mind.

She drank several cups of black coffee and chewed at a piece of toast and then let herself out of the house early, unable to bear the thought of bumping into either Lucas or Vanessa.

When Penny arrived Alina was sitting dejectedly at the back of the shop. 'Heavens, you look as though you haven't slept a wink! What's happened?'

Alina grimaced ruefully. 'I haven't! I had a row with Lucas.'

'He was waiting up to continue his hands-off Bruce Holden campaign?'

'Something like that,' agreed Alina.

Penny took off her jacket and filled the kettle. 'Want to tell me about it?'

How could she without giving herself away? 'There's nothing to tell,' she said quietly. 'But one thing's for certain, Lucas Delgado is not going to rule me. I'm seeing Bruce whether he likes it or not.'

Calmly Penny made the tea and handed Alina a cup. 'Do you think that's wise?' She sat down beside her. 'Don't you think you'll be making a rod for your own back?'

Alina frowned. 'In what way?'

Penny said, 'I've been around a lot longer than you, Alina. I've made it a habit to study people. 'You're using Bruce, aren't you?'

'What makes you say that?' Alina sipped her tea and

tried to look unconcerned. 'He's nice, I like him—why shouldn't we be friends?'

'No reason at all,' smiled the older woman. 'Except that it's Lucas you love. I'm right, aren't I? And that's why you're going against his wishes, a sort of defence mechanism because he loves Vanessa and not you.'

Alina put her cup down. 'I didn't realise I was so obvious.'

'Only to me,' smiled Penny, patting her hand. 'I have two daughters and I've gone through it all with them. But things have a way of sorting themselves out—and then you'll wonder why you made such a fuss. How long have you known you loved him?'

'For ever,' smiled Alina ruefully. 'At least, it seems like that. I suppose I was about fourteen when I first realised that my feelings towards him had changed, that I no longer saw him as a brother.'

'And did Lucas know?'

'Oh, yes!' She sounded suddenly bitter. 'He knew all right. We were going to get married. My parents didn't approve of our relationship, at least my mother didn't, so we planned to run away on my sixteenth birthday.'

'And?' prompted Penny, when Alina became suddenly silent.

'Things didn't work out,' she said limply, unable to tell her the complete truth.

Penny looked as though she understood. 'Perhaps neither of you were ready? You were very young, and men—well, they take longer than us to grow up.'

'He's ready now.' Alina's big brown eyes filled with sadness. 'He admitted last night that he's going to marry Vanessa.'

Penny was silent for a moment, then she said, 'I still don't see that that's enough reason to encourage Bruce.'

'Bruce and I are kindred souls. He's been divorced recently, but I think that deep down he still loves his wife.'

Penny smiled wryly. 'So you're both seeking comfort?'

'You could say that. I certainly need someone right now to take my mind off Lucas. The funny part about it is that I like Vanessa. We've become good friends.'

'The problem being that you're having difficulty in hiding the fact that you love her man?'

Alina grimaced. 'I don't think there's any danger of her finding out. She knows how much he irritates me with his high-handed way of running Wythenhall Manor. In fact we have quite a laugh behind his back.'

A customer put a stop to their conversation and after that they both carefully avoided talking about Lucas.

In the café at lunchtime they met Flo. She was pleased to see Alina fit and well again and asked whether her endeavours to put in a few words in the right places had helped trade.

'It's certainly booming,' said Alina. 'And if it's due to you then you have my eternal thanks.'

Flo beamed. 'It's the least I can do for all the trouble I've caused.'

Later, Alina explained to Penny what it was all about, saying how she had thought Lucas was to blame. 'I still haven't apologised,' she admitted.

'Don't you think you ought?' asked Penny. 'At least it might ease some of the tension between you.'

'But it won't give me Lucas,' grumbled Alina. 'So what's the point? Unless the opportunity presents itself I'm certainly not going to go out of my way to tell him.'

Alina dressed carefully for her date with Bruce, realising that she was doing it more out of defiance towards Lucas than because she wanted to impress, but Bruce wouldn't know that—and he would be pleased that she had taken so much trouble.

Her green suit was smart and sophisticated and she fixed her hair up on top, more than satisfied with her appearance.

She had arranged to meet Bruce downstairs at half past seven, and it was a shock to see Lucas standing there, looking as though he too was ready for an evening out. Smiling succinctly, she willed Bruce to hurry up.

After she had paced impatiently for a few seconds Lucas said grimly, 'Bruce isn't coming! He's busy!'

She stared, for a moment or two uncomprehending, then gasped. 'You did this! You've arranged it deliberately. How dare you! Bruce is as much entitled to time off as anyone.'

'Bruce takes his time off when I tell him,' he said coldly, slipping an arm beneath her elbow. 'Shall we go?'

Alina twisted away savagely. 'And what's that supposed to mean? I'm going nowhere with you!'

His dark brows rose mockingly. 'It would be such a pity to sit at home now that you've taken the trouble to dress up in your finery.'

'I'd rather do that than be forced to suffer your company,' she snapped, heading for the stairs. How could he have thought she would go out with him after the way he had behaved last night?

But she should have known she would not get away with it. In two strides he had caught up with her, his lean fingers mercilessly gripping her arm, whipping her round, compelling her to face him. 'You're coming out with me!' There was an inflexible hardness in his brown cold eyes. 'You have no choice!'

Alina drew in a deep breath, held his gaze for

several defiant seconds, then visibly gave up the struggle. 'I shall never forgive you for this, Lucas. Your methods are despicable!'

'But they get results!' He smiled calmly. 'Are you ready?'

This time she allowed him to lead her out of the house and into his waiting car. She sat like a robot, staring directly ahead, doing her very best to ignore him.

It was difficult, though. As much as she resented him at this moment, his sexual magnetism came across in waves so strong that they threatened to consume her. Every nerve-end responded and deep down she knew that an evening out with Lucas was infinitely more preferable to one with Bruce.

He took her to a quiet restaurant some miles away. It was one that she knew well by sight but had never patronised. Lucas, however, seemed perfectly familiar with his surroundings, and she couldn't help wondering whether he had brought Vanessa here. The thought didn't do her already bruised feelings much good. In fact it served to increase her black mood, and she responded to Lucas's polite conversation monosyllabically.

'Is it me,' he asked sharply at length, 'or would you have treated Bruce with the same degree of boredom?'

'I was looking forward to Bruce's company,' she retorted acidly. 'And I think you behaved abominably in not allowing him to tell me for himself that he wouldn't be able to take me out this evening.'

His lips twisted wryly. 'And then I wouldn't have had the pleasure of taking you by surprise and escorting you myself.'

'You can't tell me you're enjoying this?' she flashed.

'Not yet,' he agreed, 'but you'll thaw out, and who knows, you might amaze yourself and discover that you're really having quite a splendid time.'

'I doubt it,' she thrust bitterly. All that was in the past. Enjoying herself with Lucas was a delight never to be tasted again. In fact she could not understand why he bothered with her now—unless it was to get at Bruce! Otherwise he would surely have given Vanessa his undivided attention.

Thinking of the redhaired girl made her ask, 'Does Vanessa know you're out with me?'

A slow amused smile spread across his handsome face. 'Vanessa's an exceptional girl. She accepts my life-style. When I get back she'll want to know all about our evening together.'

The girl's a fool! thought Alina. It must indeed be an extraordinary relationship if she could allow Lucas to go out with other women—and still welcome him back! She must be very sure of him. 'Does she know that you deliberately prevented Bruce from seeing me?'

Carelessly he shrugged his broad shoulders. 'I don't know whether he's told her. In point of fact they're working together, they're going over the mailing lists. He has plenty of suggestions on where we should advertise. He's an enthusiastic man—I like him. He should be an asset, provided he doesn't do anything silly.'

'Like becoming involved with me?' she ventured heatedly. 'You should have thought of that before bringing him here.'

His face set in a tight mask. 'I had no idea that he'd make a grab at the first available woman.'

Alina found the innuendo insulting. 'I am not available, Lucas—to Bruce, or anyone. I need a friend, and Bruce needs one too, and that's all we would be.'

She might have saved her breath. He didn't believe

her. In fact he laughed in her face, a mirthless hollow sound that made her even angrier.

'You can't seriously expect me to believe that?'

'I wouldn't expect you to believe anything,' she raged. 'But it's a mistake, judging people by your own standards. They're not all like you—thank goodness!'

His lips thinned. 'You haven't always thought that way.'

'Because,' she said sweetly, 'I at one time thought you were perfect. It shows how immature I was.'

'And now you're counting your blessings that you didn't get stuck with me for the rest of your life?' The chiselled planes of his face became taut, though she couldn't think why he was angry. Only the other day he had more or less been congratulating himself on his narrow escape.

'It could have been disaster,' she admitted, relieved when the waiter interrupted their conversation. She had hardly tasted her avocado and felt even less like the fillet steak now placed before her.

Lucas, on the other hand, tucked into his meal heartily, appearing not to notice that hers lay untouched on her plate. 'The food's good here,' he said, 'but Danny's beats it. I think we were fortunate to get him.'

'*You* were fortunate,' she said bitterly. 'It had nothing to do with me. All I've done is supply the house. So far as everything else is concerned I've not been consulted once.'

He looked startled. 'It's all in the contract!'

'Then why say *we*?' she flung crossly. 'It's your baby, this. You've taken over.'

'And you take exception?' His voice had softened, for a moment he looked sad.

Alina eyed him warily. She didn't want him to understand how she felt. She wanted a full-scale argument. 'Isn't it natural that I should?'

'Perfectly natural,' he said easily, 'but I don't want you to. What I've done is for the best in the long run. One day you will again be a very rich woman.'

She picked up her knife and attacked her steak furiously. 'It's unfair, you doing all the spade-work and me simply reaping the profits.'

He looked amused. 'Well, there's a change of heart! In the first place you accused me of getting the better half of the deal. Now you've changed your tune completely. Why?'

Alina did not know why. She felt confused. She was in such a state that she didn't know what she was saying—and it was Lucas's fault! She shook her head so wildly that the pins came out and her heavy hair tumbled about her flushed face. 'Why did you insist on bringing me out tonight?'

Lucas reached out and touched her hair, running his fingers through its silky length. 'That's much better.' His voice was low and vibrant. 'You look far more like the Alina I know. And I brought you here because I wanted to. Isn't that sufficient reason?'

The back of his hand caressed her cheek. The sweet agony of his touch tortured her heart. She wondered whether he knew what he was doing, whether his actions were a deliberate attempt to arouse her, another ploy to keep her mind off Bruce Holden.

But for the moment it did not matter, she was succumbing as surely as he had said she would. The soft lights and intimate atmosphere set the seduction scene perfectly. She felt as though she was in a hypnotic trance, aware that her parted lips and half-closed eyes told their own story. How the evening finished depended on her.

CHAPTER EIGHT

'I'M glad you're relaxing.' Lucas's voice gentled into Alina's mind. 'I don't like it when you're hard. It doesn't suit you. This is how you should always be, soft and warm and very feminine.' He touched her lips with his fingertips, each feather-light movement an intimate caress.

Unable to stop herself, Alina took his hand, kissing the palm and each finger in turn, pressing it to her cheek, turning glowing eyes to his face.

'I don't think I can eat any more,' he said gruffly. 'Shall we leave?'

All Alina could do was nod. Tomorrow she would be ashamed of herself, but tonight, with Lucas looking at her like this, how could she resist?

He paid the bill and they left the restaurant hand in hand. The dark velvet sky was spangled with stars, the moon beamed approvingly, and they had all the time in the world.

He drove to a secluded spot in the middle of nowhere. Turning off the engine, he reclined their seats and gathered her unprotesting body into his arms. Alina felt weak and breathless, and wondered whether she was going out of her mind.

But hungry kiss followed hungry kiss, both of them urgent in their desire for satisfaction. She sensed a certain restraint on Lucas's part and felt grateful that he was allowing her to set the pace.

She wondered why he hadn't taken her back to the Manor, but guessed it was because of Vanessa. This

was certainly one thing he would not be discussing
with her tonight!

It had been so long since she had been in his arms
like this that her desperate need of him welled.
Feverishly she unbuttoned her jacket and placed his
hand on her breast. 'Love me, Lucas! Love me—
please!'

His smothered groan sounded anguished. Alina's
head fell back, her tongue moistening her lips, her
breathing ragged. This was the moment she had been
waiting for ever since he returned.

When he suddenly moved away, saying sharply,
'Get up!' it was like a slap on the face. Her eyes shot
wide and she wondered what she had done. In the dim
light she could faintly make out the tight anger on his
face.

'I can't do this to you,' he said thickly. 'You don't
know what you're asking.'

'I do,' whispered Alina. For the moment she didn't
care. Nothing mattered except her overpowering
desire for Lucas. He couldn't turn her on like this and
then leave her stone cold. He couldn't!

'Tomorrow you'd hate me even more.' His hands
gripped the wheel.

She sat up beside him and slid her arm around his
shoulders. 'Lucas, please——'

But he pushed her away angrily. 'Goddammit,
woman, can't you leave me alone? Can't you see that
there's no point in any of this? Make yourself decent,
for pity's sake, and let's get the hell out of here!'

Tears of self-pity flooded Alina's eyes. He wouldn't
be able to do this if he really cared. It was yet more
proof that he was following the natural urge of any man
under the circumstances.

'You're hateful!' she slung tearfully, fastening her
buttons.

Lucas smiled grimly. 'I knew you'd say that. But if I were you I'd thank your lucky stars. You might not get away so lightly another time.'

'Don't worry,' she snapped, 'there's no chance of that. No one makes a fool of me twice!'

'And you think that's what I've done?'

'You've humiliated me!' she screamed. 'You've proved conclusively that you have no interest in me. Do you know what that does for a girl's ego?'

'And I thought I was being a gentleman!' He started the engine. 'Don't forget, Bruce isn't like me. He hasn't had a woman in over twelve months. He won't back off if you offer yourself to him.'

Alina glanced across angrily. 'Perhaps I shan't want him to. He's attractive, and what's more, he finds me attractive too.' She tugged a comb through her hair and glared.

His jaw tightened grimly. 'If I thought you meant that, Alina, I'd get rid of him tonight.'

'I do mean it.' She lifted her chin defiantly, aching with love, yet desperate to hurt him as he had hurt her.

With surprising speed his hands shot out and grabbed her shoulders. 'Tell me you don't.'

The soft menace in his tone thrilled Alina, made her even more anxious to goad him. 'How can I?' she whispered, allowing the tip of her tongue to run provocatively over her lips. 'It's been a long time for me too since I went out with a man. I am a woman after all, Lucas, with a woman's desires and a woman's feelings. If you don't want me, I'm sure that Bruce——'

She got no further. His hand stung her face. 'You little bitch! You cheap little bitch!' The next second his mouth fixed on hers and it was Alina who was fighting him off.

'Damn you, Lucas!' she grated, managing to break free for a moment. But his hungry passion flooded into her and in no time at all she was melting in his arms, anger forgotten, renewed desire consuming her over-heated body.

With an angry gesture he thrust her away, slamming the car into gear and driving along the narrow road at breakneck speed.

Alina trembled and shivered and sat in her corner, wondering what the outcome of all this would be. She dared not look at Lucas. She could imagine the grimness, sensed his barely-controlled anger, and knew that she had brought it all on herself.

They reached Wythenhall Manor without one word being spoken. Lucas dropped her off outside and while he garaged his car she went up to her flat. She felt miserable and sorry for herself, and wondered why she had done it.

The next morning Penny told Alina that this would be her last day. 'Lucas came to see me. He says that now you're better there's no point in my remaining, and since he has to go to London today he can give me a lift.'

'He's going to London? He never told me!' Alina did not realise how sharp her response was.

Penny smiled. 'Lucas is very much a spur-of-the-moment man. I doubt he knew himself until the last minute.'

Or maybe she herself had driven him away! The thought made Alina incredibly sad.

While they sipped their inevitable cup of tea Penny said, 'I almost forgot—how did your date with Bruce go? You look as though you had a late night, if you don't mind me saying so.'

Alina smiled wryly. 'He had to work!'

'Lucas's doing?' Penny's fine brows rose. 'I half

expected it. So what did you do to make you look so tired?'

'Lucas took me out.'

Penny gasped. 'Do go on, I'm intrigued. How about Vanessa?'

'Precisely what I asked. Apparently she didn't mind. She and Bruce were working, would you believe? God, that's loyalty for you! I'm glad he's not my boss.'

'And was the evening a success?'

Alina wished she hadn't asked. 'No,' she said abruptly. 'And I'd rather not discuss it, if you don't mind. It was a terrible fiasco and I'm glad he's going to London. I hope I never see him again!'

'Oh!' said Penny. 'I'm sorry about that, I really am.' She took their cups through to the back and picking up a duster began polishing the furniture, looking anxiously at Alina from time to time.

The day dragged, there were few customers, and because they were both careful to avoid mentioning Lucas, there was not the easy friendship between them that was usual.

As it drew near to closing time, Alina said, 'I shall miss you. It's nice having company here.' But more than that, she knew that when she was alone again she would have nothing to take her mind off Lucas.

'I'll keep in touch,' smiled Penny, 'and I'll come and see you when I have my annual holidays.'

Alina knew that she would. Penny was not the type to make idle promises.

'And you must also come to me,' she continued. 'You'll be more than welcome—I miss not having my daughters around.'

At a minute to five Lucas came and looked expectantly at Penny. 'Are you ready?'

She nodded. 'We can pick up my case on the way.'

Alina scuttled into the back room, unable to face him, yet at the same time wanting to feast her eyes on his magnificent body. He wore an impeccably cut suit in slate grey, with a navy silk shirt, and black Gucci shoes, and he looked every inch the successful man he was.

She began washing cups that did not need washing, and jumped visibly when his voice sounded behind her. 'Are you avoiding me, Alina?'

Reluctantly she turned, amazed to see that he was smiling and relaxed. She flushed beneath the intensity of his gaze and was about to make some heated retort when she remembered Penny. 'Why should I do that?' she asked sweetly, her heart beating a tattoo within her breast.

'You could be ashamed.'

She was, but she certainly wouldn't admit it. 'I'm not,' she said with quiet defiance.

His eyes narrowed. 'Perhaps it was too much to expect?' A pulse jerked in his jaw. 'It's a pity you've changed, Alina. Perhaps one day I'll find out what happened to the sweet girl I once loved.'

'Loved?' she cried furiously, forgetting Penny, conscious only of a desire to hit back. 'You don't know the meaning of the word.'

'Well, I'm damn sure you don't,' he grated. 'Lust is perhaps more appropriate. You shocked me last night. Now I really know what sort of a girl you've become.'

Alina closed her eyes, unable to bear seeing his cold condemnation. 'Please go,' she whispered, 'and don't ever come back.'

'Oh, no!' His voice was in her ear now, his thigh brushing hers, so that her limbs quivered uncontrollably. 'You're not going to get rid of me. I intend witnessing the mess you make of your life with Bruce Holden. And I shall take the greatest delight in saying

I told you so, but don't expect me to stay around to pick up the pieces. Once I've witnessed your destruction then, and only then, shall I go.'

Alina clapped her hands to her ears, tears streaming down her cheeks. She could not take any more. Surely she did not deserve this? What had she done, except offer herself to him, to the man she loved? Was that such a crime?

'That's right, cry,' Lucas sneered. 'Weep until you can weep no more. Suffer until your heart feels like breaking—and even then you won't have experienced one half of what I've gone through!'

He spun his heel and disappeared, and Alina knew she would never forget until her dying day the look of utter loathing on his face. Her legs crumpled and she slid to the floor as harsh sobs destroyed her body.

Penny popped her head in. 'Goodbye, Alina—oh, heavens, whatever's the matter?' But the next second she was dragged backwards and Alina heard Lucas rasp, 'Leave her, she'll be all right.'

The door slammed and she was alone, but it was a long time before she moved. A paralysis took hold of her. She felt stone cold, as though she was dead, yet her mind was still alive, and round and round in her head raced Lucas's words.

When at last she was able to think coherently she began to wonder what he had meant. How had he suffered? And why, why, why did he apparently lay the blame on her? Or was it simply that she was a convenient whipping post?

Hadn't Penny said that some woman had let him down badly? Perhaps he now classed all the female sex the same, and had been waiting his opportunity to reap revenge? But why choose her when he had already caused her enough suffering? It made not one atom of sense; it merely proved how perverted he had become.

She locked up and drove home, and on the way up to her flat she met Bruce. She wished she hadn't, because she wanted to be alone. His smile was apologetic. 'Alina, about last night. Did Lucas explain?'

'I know he deliberately prevented you seeing me,' she said vehemently.

He looked shocked by her anger. 'Not deliberately. There was more to do than I'd anticipated. But tonight I'm free.' His eager smile chased away the frown.

Alina did not care what Bruce said. Lucas *had* done it on purpose, apparently being so devious about it that this nice man had not suspected. She tried to return his smile, but it was a weak attempt. 'I'm tired, Bruce. Another time, perhaps?'

He was at once all concern. 'You do look all in. Let me come and fix your meal. You can have a bath and put your feet up. I know Sally always says that——' He stopped, looking sheepish. 'Sorry, I still can't get used to the fact that she's not part of my life. But I really would like to help. I can cook—not up to Danny's standard, but I make quite a passable omelette. We could have chips with it and a glass of something. Oh, you don't drink, do you? And hell, I'm talking too much. I'm out of practice chatting up a girl, Alina, you'll have to forgive me.'

Perhaps, she decided suddenly, it would be better after all to have Bruce's company rather than sit on her own, moping. Her depression would deepen and she would be fit company for no one by morning.

'You're on,' she said, this time managing to smile more convincingly. 'But I'm out of eggs, so it will have to be sausage or liver. Can you do something with them?'

'Show me the frying pan,' he laughed, 'and I'll try.'

Everything considered, the evening turned out to be quite enjoyable. Alina bathed and changed while Bruce took over in the kitchen, and his lighthearted inconsequential conversation took her mind off her scene with Lucas.

Several times he slipped up and mentioned his wife, apologising immediately, but when Alina assured him that she did not mind, and that if he wanted to share his problems she was quite willing to listen, he relaxed, and did indeed tell her some of what had been going on between them.

She had gone off with another man and given Bruce clear grounds for divorce. 'But I'd have her back,' he said, 'even now. If she called me tomorrow I'd go running. Call me a fool if you like, but that's how it is.' Then he grinned. 'That doesn't stop me liking you, though. I meant it when I said you were one beautiful, desirable female. I don't intend remaining celibate on the offchance that Sally might one day want me back.'

Alina felt sorry for him. 'So long as you don't expect too much. I need a friend, not a lover. If that's what you're after we'd better call it a day here and now.'

Bruce took her hand, gently stroking her fingers. 'I shall never press you, Alina, into giving anything you don't want. There's something troubling you deeply, I know. If you want to discuss it, okay; if you don't, then that's okay too.'

Her smile trembled and she kissed his cheek lightly. 'Thanks, Bruce. One day I might need to take you up on that.' But not now. It was too fragile and raw, and all she needed was protection.

As though aware of this Bruce slipped his arm about

her shoulders, and she lay against him, feeling for the moment safe and secure. It was rarely one met a man such as Bruce. She felt she could trust him with her secret, open her heart and get understanding.

The next day was Saturday and the shop was fairly busy, and on Sunday Vanessa tapped on her door and asked whether they could spend the day together.

'I've finished the work Lucas left,' she said. 'And frankly I'm lonely. Bruce and Danny have gone off somewhere. Everything's ready and it seems pointless sitting downstairs on my own.'

Alina welcomed her. She had not been looking forward to today. It was almost twelve and she was still in her nightdress. There had seemed no point in getting up early.

'When's Lucas coming back?' she called from her bedroom as she changed, desperately needing to know, but reluctant to face Vanessa as she asked.

'Tomorrow,' called Vanessa, 'and heavens, don't I miss him! The place is dead when he's not here. But he wouldn't miss opening day for anything. We have our first influx of delegates tomorrow, did you know?'

Alina popped her head round the door, a jumper pulled half over her face. 'No, I didn't. No one tells me anything.'

'Not even Bruce?' asked Vanessa mischievously. 'I understand he was up here for several hours on Friday night.'

'And it was all perfectly above board,' retorted Alina. 'Ask him yourself if you don't believe me.'

'Oh, I have,' returned the redhead. 'It was just that I didn't believe him.' She sat on the floor, her knees pulled up to her chin. 'Do you like him? Really like him, I mean? I thought it was pretty awful of Lucas to bawl him out like he did in front of everyone.'

Alina sprawled on the settee, her cord-clad legs

outstretched, her hands behind her head. 'Lucas is pretty awful anyway. And I'm sorry to have to say that to you, but it's true. He's unbearable lately. I don't know how you put up with him, I really don't.'

'I've learned to accept him.' Vanessa's perfectly bowed lips curved into a secretive smile, her eyes looked dreamy. 'He's one hell of a man underneath that hard exterior.'

You don't have to tell me, thought Alina, I know all there is to know about Lucas. Or she thought she had—until the other day. His behaviour then had been like that of a total stranger. 'I reckon you're one of the privileged few to get through to him,' she said, 'because I certainly don't understand him. I used to know him so well, that's the funny part about it.'

'Perhaps you're not trying to understand him now,' said Vanessa. 'You've got a picture of him in your mind and you've forgotten that time brings changes. Have you ever visited a place you knew when you were a kid, only to find it looks nothing like you remembered—yet you can't understand why? It must be the same with people.'

'Then I wish he'd never come,' said Alina strongly. 'I didn't ask for his help. I'd have managed.' Brave words, she wished she meant them. Because she knew that without Lucas she would by now have been forced to sell Wythenhall Manor.

'You certainly do have it in for him.' Vanessa spoke as though she found it difficult to believe. 'Most girls I know absolutely drool at the mere sight of him. They'd die if he was actually living under the same roof!'

'It's the man beneath that counts,' scoffed Alina. 'They wouldn't find him so irresistible if they knew what he was really like. Give me Bruce any time. He's a solid dependable character with none of Lucas's superficial charm.'

Vanessa pounced. 'So you do like him! Good. You need someone to cheer you up.'

Perhaps it was wisest to let her go on thinking this, decided Alina, otherwise she could go on running down Lucas all day—and Vanessa might guess that she was not as immune to him as she made out.

Later on in the afternoon Flo put in an appearance. 'I've come to get the rooms ready,' she announced cheerfully. 'Mr Delgado asked me. And my two nieces are going to help at the tables and do some cleaning. He's ever so good to us, he really is.'

Alina was sick and fed up with hearing how wonderful he was. Off and on all day Vanessa had sung his praises, and now Flo! It was getting beyond the joke.

When Bruce and Danny returned she welcomed Bruce warmly. 'I've missed you. Where've you been? Why didn't you ask if I wanted to come too? You know it's my day off.'

His eyes brightened. 'I'm not averse to going out again, if that's what you want.' He winked at Vanessa. 'Do you reckon this is my lucky day?'

She smiled conspiratorially. 'Actually, Alina has been talking about you. It could be that you're in with a strong chance.'

Alina tossed her head, pretending indignance. 'I'll go and change. I'll meet you here in twenty minutes.'

What Vanessa did not know was how well she and Bruce understood one another. He had sensed her need to escape, and, true friend that he was becoming, had offered her his company.

Not knowing where they were going, Alina took a while to decide what to wear. Although the spring days were unusually warm it went chilly in the evenings, and she chose a woollen dress in strawberry pink, which was both warm and stylish, topping it with an off-white full length coat which she could easily slip off if she felt too hot.

Bruce smiled approvingly when she met him, and he too looked smart in a tweed suit and brown brogues. A typical country gentleman, she thought, and wondered whether the suit was new. It was hardly the sort of thing he would wear in London.

His car was not a patch on Lucas's—an old Hillman for which he apologised. 'But at least it's comfortable and reliable, and I'm reluctant to change it while it's going so well,' he said. 'Where shall we go? A drive and a drink later, or do you fancy a meal? I saw a nice place not too far away which I promised myself I'd visit some time.'

Alina settled back in her seat. 'I don't mind, Bruce. I'll leave it to you.' All that mattered was that she was out of the house, away from Vanessa's insistent chatter about Lucas. He was being shoved down her throat from all directions these days and it was driving her slowly insane.

He reached across and touched her hand. 'You're an easy person to be with, Alina. Sally always had very definite ideas what she wanted to do. Inevitably I fell in with them.'

Yet he still loved her! She sounded to Alina a very domineering woman. She stretched and smiled. 'I couldn't care less, Bruce. I really couldn't. I simply felt a desperate urge to get out of the house.'

'Perhaps it's because you've been cooped up so long with your illness?' he said. 'You're still looking peaky. What you need is a good brisk walk. We'll find a place to park by the river; it won't be dark for another hour yet.'

'Yes, doctor,' she quipped, and it felt good to have

her mind made up for her. Ever since her parents died it had been decisions all the way, and even though this was something so simple as going for a walk, she appreciated not having to think for herself.

She wondered whether Bruce would understand if she told him, then decided he would probably think she was cracking up.

It was peaceful and relaxing by the river. They watched it tumbling in cream foam over a weir, they saw it run quiet beneath overhanging bushes. In the fields tractors ploughed the light-brown soil, followed by countless crows and gulls searching for food.

A pear orchard was breaking into bud, wild primroses bloomed, Friesians grazed contentedly. In the distance mellow Cotswold-stone houses glowed beneath the westering sun and a church steeple rose proudly from their midst.

They held hands and rarely talked, and Alina felt much happier than she had for two days. Bruce would never arouse feelings in her like Lucas did, but she felt very close, and was grateful to him for bringing her out.

'Where did you go today?' she asked, as they wended their way back to his car.

He shrugged, his easy smile splitting his good-looking face. 'Here and there, meeting people, spreading the word about Wythenhall Manor.'

'Work?' She looked disbelieving. 'I thought it was your day off?'

'I'm not allowed days off, remember?' But he was laughing all the same. 'No, I happened to mention to Lucas a fellow I know who's Managing Director of a chain of companies, and he asked me to go and see him, introduce our new centre. He was quite impressed. He's coming along to have a look. If he finds it favourable he should put quite a lot of business our way.'

Lucas—always Lucas! They bent over backwards to do whatever he asked—even giving up their spare time. Vanessa, she could understand. Vanessa loved him. But Bruce? Especially after the way he had been ticked off the other night—it was quite beyond her powers of comprehension.

'I don't know why you let that man rule your life. It's not fair, working seven days a week.' She looked really cross and he stopped and stood in front of her.

'Hey, Alina, don't get so het up! I didn't do it for Lucas alone. You have half shares in it, don't forget. I did it as much for you as for him.'

He took her face between his hands. 'Come on, smile, and I'll let you into a secret.'

It was impossible not to respond. His good humour was infectious. A faint dimple showed in her cheeks. 'Go on, then,' she said, 'and it had better be good.'

'To be quite truthful, I did it only for you. I keep remembering what you said about wanting to bring your family up here, and I've made up my mind to go all out to make sure Wythenhall Manor is a success. I want it to be your home again, Alina. I want you to be rich enough to be able to run it the way it once was.'

'And do you think,' she asked wryly, 'that Lucas will give it up once it's making a profit? Don't you think he'll want to carry on? I don't know how rich he is, but the way I see it, making money is a mania with him.'

'He has the Midas touch,' admitted Bruce. 'He's shrewd and has the uncanny ability of always knowing where to invest wisely. But he's fair. I can't see him hanging on to it just to spite you.'

You don't know Lucas, she thought, but what were they doing talking about Lucas when the very reason behind her coming out was to escape him? She shrugged and said, 'That remains to be seen. Let's find that place you were on about. I'm suddenly starving!'

Bruce looked thoughtful as they walked the last few yards and Alina wondered whether she hadn't been too vehement talking about Lucas. She didn't want Bruce guessing her true feelings.

The hotel was warm and cheerful with the inevitable smell of burning logs. She slipped off her coat and sipped orange juice and smiled at Bruce, thanking him for bringing her.

Later they ate and listened to some folk singers who had arrived to brighten up the evening. The dining room was cosy with a red carpet and mirrored walls, and red-shaded lamps on each table.

Alina relaxed and forgot Lucas, and Bruce soon had her laughing. He had a fund of funny stories and the next hour passed quickly. They were waiting for their coffee when she suddenly had a most peculiar feeling that someone was watching her.

Cold shivers ran down her spine and through the mirror behind Bruce she focused on Lucas. He was with Vanessa, but his attention was on herself, cold disapproval very apparent on his handsome tanned face.

Their eyes met and he inclined his head in a mock salute before turning his attention back to his companion.

After that it was difficult to ignore him, and time and time again Alina found her eyes drawn towards his reflection. Vanessa looked if possible more beautiful than ever this evening. She wore a flamboyant red dress which contrasted strangely with her copper hair, but which surprisingly looked exactly right.

Their conversation seemed to be very private and very intimate, and Alina felt jealousy gnawing inside her. Coffee arrived and she sipped it gratefully, glad of something to distract her attention.

'Is something wrong?' Bruce noticed her agitation.

She could have said, 'Oh, yes, he's right in the room behind me.' But she didn't. If Bruce saw Lucas there was a strong possibility he would invite him to join them. Alina did not feel she could stand that. Instead she put her hand across the table, needing the physical comfort of this dependable man.

He smiled warmly, anxiously, and squeezed her hand. 'Do you want to go?'

That would mean they would have to walk right past Lucas's table. On the other hand, Vanessa and Lucas were only just beginning their main course. It could be a long and uncomfortable wait.

She nodded. 'When you've finished your coffee.' She made herself speak calmly and sip her drink slowly, whereas in fact her nerves were screaming and she wanted to tear out of the restaurant. Lucas's condemnation made itself felt even from this distance.

The next ten minutes seemed the longest Alina had ever spent, and when Bruce finally said he was ready she jumped up quickly, tipping over her chair in her haste, then swinging round an catching a cup with the handle of her bag.

The eyes of the room were upon them. Scarlet-cheeked, she allowed Bruce to escort her towards the door. For one moment she thought they were going to make their escape without Lucas saying anything. He was speaking to Vanessa as they passed his table. Bruce, surprisingly, did not see him, and Alina guessed he was anxious to leave after the embarrassment of her accident.

But as relief began to flood over her she felt her

hand caught in a merciless grip. She glanced at him sharply, yanking herself free, smiling weakly at Vanessa.

His eyes were like chips of ebony in a granite setting. He grabbed her hand again and pulled her down so that her ear was on a level with his mouth. 'The road to destruction has begun,' he whispered harshly. 'Why don't you back out before it's too late?'

'And why don't you mind your own damn business!' she cried, then ran from the room appalled as she realised she had said it loud enough for everyone to hear.

Bruce had disappeared. She wondered whether he would ever ask her out again.

CHAPTER NINE

ALINA had climbed into Bruce's car and sat there for several minutes before he asked what was wrong.

'Didn't you see Lucas?' There was a mixture of shock and pain on her face, and her voice barely rose above a whisper.

'In the restaurant? No!' He frowned. 'Was that where you got to? Heavens, he must think me frightfully rude, walking out like that without a word, but I was——'

She reached across and touched his arm. 'Embarrassed because of what I did?'

He relaxed and smiled. 'Embarrassed for you, not because of you. What did he have to say? Something pretty devastating, by your expression.'

Alina sighed deeply, compressing her lips. 'I hate that man!'

Bruce looked shocked by the violence of her words. He took her hand urgently between his own. 'You're overreacting. If he told you off for making a scene, forget it. He's something of a perfectionist. He once said to me that he never suffers fools. I expect he thought you should have been more careful.'

'Maybe I should have,' she said miserably, feeling suddenly drained. 'Take me home, Bruce. I've had enough.'

Appreciating her need for silence, Bruce did not speak until they arrived back at the manor. 'You really shouldn't let Lucas get through to you,' he said, pushing the door and standing back for her to enter. 'If he knows he's upsetting you, he'll take advantage.

He prefers a woman with spirit, someone who'll stand up to him.' He smiled grimly. 'I've seen him in operation enough times to know it works.'

'You reckon that's why he and Vanessa get on so well?'

'Vanessa's one in a million. She understands him like no other woman ever has. If he marries her he'll be losing the best p.a. he's ever had, or likely to get.'

There was no if about it, Alina thought dismally. It was fact. And the more she thought about it the more cut up she became. At the door to her flat she said, 'Would you like to come in? It's too early yet for bed and pointless the two of us sitting about on our own.' Besides which she did not want time to think.

Bruce needed no second asking. He took off his jacket and sat himself down, ironically on the same chair Lucas had used that first time he had visited her. There was no comparison between the two men. Bruce was cheerful and comfortable, good company but never exciting.

Lucas in that chair had set her pulses racing, and it was no good telling herself that it was not he she would have preferred there now. Not in one of his hateful antagonising moods, but as she had once known him—loving, considerate, and very, very desirable.

'What are you thinking?'

Alina had been unaware that her gaze was fixed on Bruce. Mentally shaking herself back to the present, she smiled wryly. 'I'm sorry, I was——' She stopped herself just in time. She had been about to say that she wished he was someone else. How awful if she had! What would he think? She really ought not to let Lucas take over her mind like this.

'I was miles away,' she finished lamely.

'You were thinking of Lucas?'

His uncanny perception startled her. 'How did you know?'

'You've not been the same since you spotted him in the restaurant.' Bruce loosened his tie and studied her thoughtfully. 'You'd seen him earlier? That was why you were desperate to leave? Why didn't you tell me?'

'Because——' She wondered how much he knew. 'Because I thought you might invite him over to our table—and I don't think I could have stood that.' Please, God, don't let him guess the truth. His pity was the last thing she wanted. It hurt enough to know she loved a man who was going to marry someone else, without it becoming common knowledge.

He pushed himself up and came over to the settee where she sat. His kind face was full of concern. 'I wish I understood. He's a good man, Alina, and in his own way he's helping you. Don't hate him so. I can't bear seeing you unhappy.'

She grimaced and pulled him down beside her. 'I don't enjoy it. I simply can't help myself. He's got beneath my skin and——'

He silenced her with a gentle finger on her lips. 'Shh, sweetheart!' And he coaxed her into the crook of his arm. 'Relax and forget Lucas. This is Bruce, remember, your friend?' His easy grin was difficult to resist. 'Lucas won't always be here, he has other interests to consider, but I will, and I'm not going to have my pleasure spoiled by your miserable little face.'

Lifting her chin with his finger, he dared her to defy him. 'Come on, smile!' And when she obeyed—weakly, but a smile nevertheless, he said, 'That's better. Now make sure that it's there every time we meet. No more blue devils. He's your partner, an equal. You're as good as him any day. Never let him get you down again. Promise?'

If only it were that easy! If there were no emotions

involved she could stand up to Lucas as well as the next man. But when her heart felt as though it had been wrenched from her body and trodden on, it was difficult to put on a brave face.

Impulsively she kissed Bruce's cheek. 'I don't know what I'd do without you.'

'Know something? Neither do I.' He took her face between his hands, still smiling, but his eyes were for once serious.

She knew he was going to kiss her, that her warmth had provoked feelings he generally kept suppressed. She also knew that it would be unnecessarily cruel to stop him. But although she tried to work up some enthusiasm her response was pathetic, and with a sigh he gently put her from him. 'I'm sorry, Alina. I should have known better.'

'I'm sorry too,' she whispered. 'I don't like doing this to you, Bruce. I did warn you.'

'Is there someone else?' It was the first time he had questioned her private life.

She could not lie. She nodded. 'But he doesn't love me.'

Never down for long, Bruce grinned. 'Then I'm in with a chance?'

She brushed a strand of hair from her eye, looking at him sadly from beneath her thick lashes. 'I wish I could say yes, but I'm not the sort of person to build up a man's hopes for nothing. I'm sorry, Bruce.'

He squeezed her comfortingly. 'It wouldn't work anyway. There'll always be Sally. I don't know what I'm after. Not an affair, it wouldn't seem right, it would be like—letting her down!'

After what she had done to him! He really was an exceptional man. Alina wished she could love him, he deserved a better deal than the one he had got.

'We're friends,' she said, 'and that means a lot to me

right now.' And she was thankful Bruce had not pressed for more details.

They remained in each other's arms for a long time, occasionally speaking, for the most content in companionable silence. And Bruce's calming influence settled Alina so that by the time he suggested making a move she really felt much better.

His tie had come off by this time and now he draped it round his neck like a scarf, and hooking his jacket with a finger he slung it over one shoulder. In the doorway he turned, pressing a light kiss to her forehead. 'Thanks, Alina, for your company—and I'm sorry—about the man you love. He must be a fool.'

It was she who was the fool, she thought, as she slowly undressed and hung up her clothes. She should never have let Lucas come back into her life. She ought to have foreseen what would happen and got rid of him at once. Thank goodness it was Monday tomorrow. There was a sale on in Cheltenham, she would be too busy to spare him a thought.

It was a distinct shock, therefore, when she saw his familiar fair head inches above everyone else, weaving its way towards her through the crowded sale room.

Unreasonable panic took hold of her and she looked around for an avenue of escape. But it was a popular sale and she was hemmed in. She had not Lucas's physical strength to push her way through. And even if she did try she had no doubt that he would catch up with her.

'What are you doing here?' she demanded, the moment he reached her.

He looked amused, his eyes crinkling at the corners as he smiled, his mobile lips parting to reveal his very white teeth. 'The same as you, I would imagine. There are a few pieces that I'm particularly interested in.'

The crowd pressed her against him and it was

impossible to ignore his firm length. The contact sent her head spinning and she waved her programme feebly as she tried to push herself away. But Lucas imprisoned her hands, holding them down at her sides. 'Why struggle, when you know as well as I that there's no escape?'

Not from him, that was an indisputable fact. No matter how many miles parted them he was still there in her mind, possessing her soul, disturbing every hour of every day.

But surely there was escape from this room? Frantically she looked about her, but his breadth and height blocked her view, and the male smell of him filled her nostrils, until in the end she did not want to move.

She liked it here beside him. She revelled in the heady intoxication of his long lean thighs against her own, the quiet thudding of his heart, and she wanted to close her eyes and wrap her arms about him, forgetting everyone else, blissfully concentrating on the physical exhilaration she was experiencing.

But because she knew this was impossible, because she knew it was pure insanity standing there unresisting, she dropped her head back and looked up into his face. It seemed yards above her, a cruel gleam darkening his eyes. 'You shouldn't be here,' she declared strongly. 'Vanessa said you wanted to be at the official opening.'

'It's already happened,' he said softly. 'On the dot of nine the first delegates streamed in, and we had a champagne reception. They were very impressed.'

Alina stiffened, struggling to put inches between them, finding it impossible because of the density of the crowd. Resentment flooded her, and she fought for the right words. 'You have a nerve! Aren't I your partner? Why wasn't I invited?'

The thick dark brows rose into the thatch of strongly waving blond hair. 'You look surprised—I can't think why. You've always made a point of telling me you don't drink.'

'It's not the champagne that bothers me,' she cried, 'but I had no idea you were going to make such a song and dance about it, and considering that it is, or was, my home, I do think I should have been involved in the ceremony.'

His smile was a little too casual. 'You're forgetting our agreement.'

'To hell with that ridiculous contract!' she exclaimed angrily. 'I wish I'd never signed the damn thing. But I find it hard to believe that I now mean so little to you that you'd leave me out of an event like that. How cruel can you get?'

'No more cruel than you've been to me,' Lucas said tightly, 'and I suggest you quieten your voice. You're attracting a great deal of attention.'

Alina shivered and lowered her eyes. There were many people here that she knew. Word would soon get round. 'Why don't you go and stand somewhere else?' she asked tiredly.

'Because I quite like it here.' He draped an arm easily about her shoulders. The auctioneer's hammer hit the table and the sale began.

Alina had marked on her programme the items in which she was interested. Looking down, Lucas said, 'Tell me how much you're prepared to go to and I'll do the bidding.' And because she could not trust herself to do anything right with him standing so painfully close, Alina did as he asked.

Whether it was because word had got round who he was, and people knew that there was not much point in going too high against him because he could easily afford to outbid the lot of them, she did not know, but what she did know was that she got what she wanted at much lower prices than she had expected to pay.

She supposed she should be grateful, but she found it difficult to thank him and her grudging, 'Thanks, Lucas,' seemed a poor return for what he had done.

He shrugged. 'It was nothing. But if you'd join me for lunch, I'd like that.'

The sale was far from over, but they had both finished their own particular business, and Alina guessed he was aware that she had someone running the shop for her so there was no need to rush back.

She nodded, and he shouldered his way through the people, the ones she knew smiling and eyeing Lucas curiously. She could imagine the number of tongues that would be wagging after the sale.

But they were the least of her worries. She had a further hour or so of Lucas's company to be got through, and it was a foregone conclusion that it would be anything but pleasant.

Ironically, he took her to the same place they had visited the evening before. Alina bit back a protest, allowing him to take her coat, and sitting demurely in her seat, her hands in her lap.

She wore a thin woollen sweater in dusky pink which clearly defined the upward thrust of her breasts, and it disconcerted her to discover Lucas insolently appraising her.

'You're right, you have grown up.' His smile was sardonic. 'Quite an improvement on the childish virgin I almost married!'

Alina said nothing, preferring to pretend he did not bother her, taking the menu from the waiter and studying it. In actual fact the words danced before her eyes, and when Lucas said quietly, 'Shall I order for you?' she was relieved.

Their first course was smoked salmon. She nibbled

her way through the wafer-thin slices of brown bread, tasted the tender pieces of fish, aware that Lucas's disturbing eyes were upon her.

The salmon was followed by duckling in a rich red wine sauce, and when it became apparent that Lucas had no further intention of baiting her Alina relaxed.

Attuned to her every mood, he smiled. 'That's better. It's amazing what good food and good company can do.'

She would have disputed the company bit, but nevertheless returned his smile. 'I agree, the food here is excellent, but I didn't know you knew this place. I was surprised to see you with Vanessa last night.'

'So I gathered.' A devilish light gleamed in his eyes. 'I know you're not usually so clumsy, and I could hardly believe that Bruce had such a devastating effect on you—so it had to be me.'

Determined not to spoil their apparent truce, Alina answered lightly, 'Such modesty!'

He grinned. 'I know myself pretty well. I also know you, Alina, better than you think.'

She wondered what that was supposed to mean. 'Should I be flattered?'

'You ought to know. We were pretty close once. Something like that doesn't disappear. Maybe it gets forgotten, pushed into the background, but it can easily be resurrected. It's almost as though I've never been away.'

Alina felt her heart begin to race. 'I wish you hadn't,' she said before she could stop herself, then felt her cheeks colour until she was sure they matched her jumper.

'I didn't have much choice.' Lucas sounded bitter. 'But as it turns out, it was all for the best. I would never be where I am today if I'd stayed here.'

'And you think that money has brought you more

happiness than marrying me would have done?' She was not accusing, merely curious. He *had* had a choice, and he had chosen freedom—at her expense.

He considered her question carefully. 'I think that when I do marry it will be—an asset, if you like, not to have to worry about money, but no—I don't think I've been any happier. I was very fond of you, Alina. Leaving you was the hardest thing I've ever had to do.'

She noted he used the past tense. 'But the other day you said it would never have worked out.'

He laughed, deep-throated genuine amusement. 'I say all sorts of things when I'm in a temper. You, above anyone, Alina, should know when I mean it.'

Maybe she should, but she was afraid she did not understand him any more. She could not understand why he was talking to her now like this. It seemed bizarre that he could discuss their relationship so apathetically. She smiled wanly and said in a tight little voice, 'I thought you meant that.'

'And did it matter to you?' He was suddenly serious.

Alina looked into the hypnotising depths of his eyes, aware that her heart was going crazy all over again. 'Yes. No woman likes to think she can't make a man happy.'

'So you're generalising?' He looked surprisingly disappointed.

And Alina felt embarrassed that she had almost given herself away. 'Tell me about yourself, Lucas,' she said urgently. 'Tell me what you've been doing all these years.' It was imperative that she move the subject away from herself.

He shrugged. 'Making money, like everyone else.'

'But how did you get going? Most people work, but they never become——'

'Millionaires,' Lucas finished for her, laughing as she gasped.

'You are—a—millionaire?' It was totally unbelievable.

'I suppose so,' he said easily. 'I've never really counted—I don't have the time. Perhaps I ought to write a book, *"How to become a millionaire in eight years."* Or, *"Finish with your woman and become a millionaire."* That would be more like it!'

'You mean I'd have held you back?'

Their eyes battled for a few moments before he laughed bitterly. 'Let's say I wouldn't have had so much incentive. I always intended becoming rich, but parting from you helped.'

'I'm glad I've been of some use,' Alina retorted stiffly, 'but I can't profess to understand.'

'That makes two of us.' Lucas leaned forward and carelessly brushed her cheek with the back of a finger. 'But if you're really interested I'll give you the bare outlines. I don't want to bore you with details.'

He would never bore her. She loved the sound of his voice, the deep timbre, every inflection. She could sit and listen to him for hours, so long as they weren't arguing!

'It didn't take me long to decide that I'd never get rich if I remained a groom all my life, so I joined a company of trouble-shooters, experts in helping other firms out of trouble. I've always had a quick mind and I soon learned how a business is run. After that I seemed to develop an instinct for nosing out trouble and what was more important, I suppose, I could usually see a way out. Within two years I'd worked my way as near to the top as I could get, so I left and set up my own company.

'I eventually employed quite a team, all hand-picked men who were as good as me, if not better. I wouldn't have accepted anything less. Some firms were so deeply in trouble that they thought I couldn't help, so I bought them out. They've all prospered.'

Alina was impressed. He was not boasting, he was stating simple facts. 'Where do the antique shops fit into all this?'

'Ah, that was slightly different, and I suppose in some obscure way you had something to do with that.'

'Me?' She was astonished. 'How?'

'Seeing your parents' lovely furniture and possessions when I worked here I developed a feeling for them that never left me. I acquired a few bits and pieces of my own which I always purchased from the same shop. An old man owned it and we developed quite a relationship. He taught me a lot about antiques. He had no family, and when he died I discovered to my surprise that he'd left his shop to me. It's the only thing I've never had to work for, and no one will ever be able to understand how much it meant to me.'

He sounded quite emotional. This was a side of Lucas that Alina did not know, and she was surprised. She smiled warmly. 'And now you have a chain of them?'

'And it's also the end of my story.' He finished the few remaining peas on his plate. 'Do you want anything else?'

'Just coffee,' she said, 'and I do appreciate your telling me. And while we're on the subject, I want to apologise for accusing you of slandering my name. Flo confessed. I'm sorry.'

A slow smile spread across his face. 'I already knew. Flo and I have quite an understanding.'

'Damn you,' she said softly, but she did not mean it, and her eyes smiled into his. 'She's also helped boost my trade. Apparently she knows quite a lot of wealthy people—I expect she's worked for them over the years.'

'I expect so.'

Lucas did not sound as though he believed it, but Alina did not care. For the moment all that mattered was that she and Lucas were getting on like a house on fire; no animosity, no hatred, no harsh words—no love! But that was something she had to accept.

She felt sad when it was time for them to leave. It was rarely these days that she and Lucas got together without arguing, and she wanted it to go on and on.

As though sensing her dejection, when she lowered herself into his gleaming silver sports car, he said, 'We'll go a ride. It's far too nice a day for you to be stuck inside that shop.'

Alina looked up at him from beneath the strands of hair which had blown across her face. His blurred outline looked mysterious and sexy as he bent low in the doorway, and she drew in a deep breath, moistening trembling lips with the tip of her tongue.

All she could do was nod; she did not trust herself to speak. Her whole body was responding to Lucas's vibrant masculinity, the clean smell of him assailed her nostrils, intoxicating her, and she willed him to step back so that she could regain her equilibrium.

But her breathing space was brief. No sooner had he moved than he was in the car beside her, his long legs stretched out, the thin material of his trousers taut across powerful muscles.

Their shoulders were virtually touching. She was aware of the warmth of him, the virile strength of him, and his sexual appeal was total. She glanced across nervously, disconcerted to discover he was looking at her. His soft brown eyes were creased at the corners, their depths held a message she was unable to interpret.

'Why are you frightened of me?' He reached across and cupped her chin, his thumb moving with the deliberate sensual strokes down the soft skin of her throat.

Unable to control the quiver of emotion his touch evoked, Alina endeavoured to jerk free, but his grip was inflexible. He smiled confidently, teeth very white against his bronzed face. 'Answer me, Alina. What is it about me that disturbs you?'

Everything, she wanted to affirm. Your body, your voice, your hypnotic eyes. There was not one inch of him that did not excite her. Even his hair; strong, wiry, possessed of a mind of its own, always escaping his attempts to tame it. She wanted to run her fingers through it, hold his head between her fingers, bring that beautiful face so close to her own that their lips met.

And as though he knew exactly what rampant thoughts chased through her mind, Lucas leaned across and with calculated slowness allowed his lips to feather her cheeks, the tip of her nose, her eyes, all the time looking at her, his eyes smouldering darkly.

It seemed a long long time before he finally reached her mouth. Alina's head had fallen back against the seat. She felt as though she was suspended in a timeless world, as though all emotion was slowly being drained out of her. Lucas was possessing her! She was giving him his answer.

She did not even realise that a sound escaped her throat when his lips briefly brushed hers in a kiss so infinitely soft and tender that it was like nothing she had ever experienced.

She expected more, she wanted more, and was filled with a searing disappointment when he sat back in his seat and started the engine. When she dared to look at him there was satisfaction on his face and her craving faded abruptly, turning to burning indignation.

'And what was all that about?' High colour warmed her cheeks, quivering fingers raked through her tousled hair.

Lucas moved out of the hotel car park and on to the open road before he answered, changing gear with slow fluid movements. Each action deliberate and controlled—the way he handled her!

His lips curved wryly as he glanced across before turning his attention back to the ribbon of road stretching out endlessly in front of them. On either side rolling uplands and lush green valley slopes were tree filled and dappled with sunlight. But for once Alina's beloved Cotswold countryside held no appeal.

'Wasn't it what you wanted?' Lucas's voice was a low growl, coming from somewhere deep in his stomach, a nerve-tingling sound that earlier would have thrilled her to the core.

In bewilderment she shook her head. 'You're destructive,' she cried. 'Heavens, you know what you do to me! Why can't you leave me alone? Aren't you satisfied with one woman?'

'Don't worry, I have no intention of going further.' There was now a hardness in his tone, his jaw had firmed, and she noticed knuckles gleaming white as he gripped the wheel.

'I merely wanted to give you a taste of the joys you might have experienced with me.' Lucas shot her a quick sidelong glance and she was shocked at the stone cold hardness of his eyes. Who would have believed they could change so rapidly?

'Tell me, what was it like with Bruce? Did his caresses turn your limbs to water? Did you almost faint with the sheer exquisite pleasure of his kisses?'

'Stop it! Stop it!' Alina clapped her hands over her ears. 'I don't want to hear any more!'

But he carried on as though she had not spoken. 'Did your body respond totally? Did you offer yourself to him like you were doing to me a few minutes ago?'

Oh, God, why was he doing this to her? 'Shut up!' she screamed wildly. 'I won't take this from you. Why can't you leave Bruce out of it?'

'Because Bruce is now very much a part of your life,' he suggested casually. 'How can we leave him out? He's your lover, isn't he? Also your executioner.' There was grim satisfaction as he uttered these final words.

Alina's lovely eyes flared brilliantly, her nostrils dilating as she strove to stop herself from hitting out. She had to curl her fingers into her palms and keep them tightly at her side. 'You are the most despicable man I have ever had the misfortune to meet!'

Her breathing became shallow and rapid and she wished they weren't driving along the road. She wanted to fling herself at him, screaming. She wanted to rake her fingers down his face and scar those damned handsome features. She wanted to leave him something to remember her by.

'Bruce is not my lover,' she said through gritted teeth.

'No?' There was a definite mocking arch to his brows. 'He looked one hell of a satisfied man when I saw him leaving your flat last night. Somewhat dishevelled too, as though he'd been having a thoroughly bawdy time.'

Alina gasped, revulsion sickening her. How could he think such a thing? In a blind fury she lost all coherent thought, releasing her seat-belt and lunging at him, her hands beating wildly, tears streaming. 'I hate you, Lucas Delgado, I hate you! I wish you were dead!'

'Alina!' His powerful voice struck into her mind. 'For God's sake, get away.'

'No!' Her nails found their target and she dragged them deeply down his cheeks, seeing the satisfying streak of red that followed. 'I'm going to disfigure you, Lucas. When I've finished with your face Vanessa won't want you.'

'*Move!*' With superhuman strength Lucas thrust her resisting body from across him. She felt her head strike the door, then just as suddenly she was flung back. The squeal of brakes sounded deafeningly loud.

A quick scared glance as she pushed herself up and she knew that no way were they going to stop before they left the road. 'Lucas! what have I done?'

For a few seconds they seemed to be sailing through the air, then they hit the grassy side of the valley with a sickening bang that shook every bone in her body. Up again they bounced before rolling over and over.

She was hurtled round and round and heard as if from a distance the thin wail of her screams, and was convinced that neither of them would come out of this alive.

Her whole life flashed before her eyes, green grass and trees flew past the windows in a blur. She yelled and clawed and panicked.

Finally, after a hundred years of falling and spinning and being constantly thrown about, the car came to a rocking, shuddering, metal-tearing halt. And then a dreadful silence. A chilling silence!

Why wasn't Lucas speaking? They had stopped, and they weren't dead. Alina was full of pain but somehow, miraculously, they had come out of this alive. So why didn't he say something?

The car had by some quirk of fate landed the right way up, and when her dizziness passed she looked across at him.

Oh, God! She couldn't bear it. His face was covered in blood and he sagged limply in his seat, held in position by the belt alone. Not the flicker of an eyelid, nothing.

She had killed him!

Nausea rose in her throat, followed by scream after hysterical scream. Mist blurred her vision. Then she was floating, floating away from it all. Perhaps she was dying too? She hoped so. She prayed so. No way could she live with the knowledge that she had caused Lucas's death.

CHAPTER TEN

ALINA heard her name repeated softly, insistently, but it was too much of an effort to respond. She was warm and comfortable and she did not want to be disturbed. Why couldn't they leave her alone?

The voice faded and the next time she heard it it was much louder, much nearer. But she couldn't open her eyes. It felt as though her lids were glued together.

'Alina, can you hear me?'

It was a woman's voice. She thought she knew it, but everything was muddled and she wanted to sleep, sleep for a very long time. She moved her head restlessly. Leave me alone.

She'd said the words, yet hadn't heard the sound of her voice. She couldn't understand it. What had happened to her?

And then someone else joined the woman. Their voices were muted, hardly discernible. Alina strained to hear what they were saying.

'I think she's coming round.'

Coming round? What did they mean? Coming round from what, from where? Her mouth was dry, terribly dry. And it was so hot. Where was she? She tried to lick her lips, but her tongue was dry too.

Someone must have noticed. A sponge moistened her lips; a gentle hand bathed the beads of perspiration from her brow, wiped the stickiness from her eyes.

She managed to flutter them open, her lids heavy so that it was an effort, and she had time only to see two blurred outlines before they fell again. She needed to rest, she was so tired, so very, very tired.

And then the haze cleared from her mind, but there was pain, terrible pain. She tried to move her legs, she tried to reach out, but her limbs were strangely heavy and wouldn't obey her command.

She opened her eyes, but shut them again quickly when she saw her legs in plaster, strung up by some strange-looking contraption. She was in hospital! She had been in an accident! But when, where?

She heard a sound and looking again saw a nurse at her side. The woman smiled. 'Hello, Alina. So you're awake at last. How are you feeling?' She bent over her and Alina had a vision of soft green eyes, the colour of spring. No, the colour of grass and leaves! For a brief space she saw mirrored in the eyes a blur of whirling greenery. A flood of agonising memories were released, and then merciful, merciful blackness once again.

It was too much to bear. She was alive, but Lucas wasn't. And without Lucas she did not want to live. She would willingly have given her life for him, but not the other way round. And she had killed him as surely as if she had driven a stake through his heart.

Hot tears escaped from her lids, rolling down her cheeks, wetting the pillow. 'Let me die,' she implored, the wavery sound of her voice filling the room. 'Please let me die.'

A hand touched her brow and her eyes shot wide. Vanessa! Lucas's fiancé! Oh, God, no! She had ruined her life too! Why was she here now? To call her a murderer, a killer? Would they send her to prison?

She stared at the redhead, unable to drag her eyes away from the lovely face which looked at her with gentle concern. Yes, concern! Not recrimination, not hatred, but compassion!

It couldn't be! Why should Vanessa feel like this? 'Vanessa?' Her softly spoken word brought a smile.

'Alina.' Vanessa's lips touched the pallid brow. 'You had us worried. How are you?'

'How am I?' How did she expect her to be? She was half crazed with pain and she hated herself—why didn't Vanessa hate her too? She smiled weakly. 'I'm not sure. My legs hurt and I ache all over.' It all sounded so banal. Why were they making pleasant conversation?

'You will. And your arms, how are they?'

Alina looked down and saw the heavily bandaged limbs lying limply at her side. 'I didn't know. I should have. Vanessa, I'm confused. I don't——'

'Shh!' Vanessa put a finger to her lips. 'It's much too soon to talk. The nurse said I could only have a couple of minutes. I'll have to go. I'll come back later. Perhaps you'll feel better.'

She wouldn't. She would never feel the same again. Apart from her injuries, whatever they were, she was numb. She had destroyed herself. When she recovered she would walk and talk and laugh, and act as though nothing was wrong. But inside her would be nothing. No mind, no feeling, nothing—except a loathing for herself for taking Lucas's life.

The next few days passed in a blur of pain and drugged sleep. Doctors and nurses appeared and disappeared. Vanessa came and went. They said little; there was nothing to say. Her life was a complete mess, Vanessa's too. They had both lost the man they loved.

But it seemed important to let Vanessa know how she felt. 'I want to thank you for being so nice,' she said one afternoon. 'I don't deserve it. You should hate me. Why don't you?'

'Hate you?' Vanessa looked puzzled. 'I think you must have hurt your head as well. Shall I fetch the doctor?'

Alina shook her head in anguish. 'Don't joke—this is important to me. Lucas is dead and it was my fault, and I can't think why you're behaving like this.' She turned her head into the pillow, fighting tears.

She felt Vanessa's hand stroking her hair. Oh, God, Vanessa, don't be nice to me, please. She wanted censure, hatred, she deserved them. She couldn't stand this gentle forgiveness.

'Alina, my dear, Lucas——'

'No, Vanessa, no!' she shrieked, hysteria suddenly rising. 'Don't say anything. Just go. Get out! Leave me alone!'

Vanessa looked startled, but reluctantly obeyed. At the door she looked back, taking a step into the room again, then changing her mind.

A nurse came shortly afterwards and gave Alina an injection. Alina looked at her blankly. 'Why don't you let me die?'

The nurse smiled. 'Because we're here to save lives, not take them. You're pretty badly knocked about, but you'll pull through. You'll sleep now, and when you wake I want no more of this nonsense.'

Alina closed her eyes. They didn't understand. No one did. No one ever would. Vanessa's calm acceptance of the situation was making her own burden all the harder to bear.

After that Lucas was never mentioned again.

Eventually the layers of bandage came off her arms. They were lacerated and bruised and had swollen to twice their normal size, but they were not broken—unlike her legs! It would be a long time before she walked again.

Her ribs and back were bruised too, but she was lucky to be alive, considering she hadn't worn her safety-belt—or so they kept telling her.

Lucky! Little did they know she would have been luckier had she not lived.

Vanessa turned up one day with a bunch of red roses. 'From Bruce,' she said grandly. 'He sends his love and he'll come when he can, but he's so busy, poor man. The centre's really taken off with a bang. Lucas——' And then she bit her lip and shut up.

What had she been going to say? Lucas would have been so proud? Lucas was confident this would happen? It was true. He would have been pleased and happy. He had planned it. He had worked at it and set it up—and now he wasn't here to witness its success.

Vanessa turned and looked out of the window, her thin shoulders bowed. Alina guessed what she was thinking. After a while she returned to the bed, her face composed, and they talked about Wythenhall Manor.

She described some of the delegates—quick, humorous word pictures that had Alina laughing. 'This one man was like a bulldog, thick and squat, but I think he saw himself as God's gift to women. I couldn't get rid of him.'

And they talked about the shop. Alina's friend in the village was coping, but Penny was arriving at the weekend to take over until Alina was better.

Alina had already had a card from her, with the message, 'I guess you only did this to get me back!'

Day followed day, each one the same as the last. Alina lost all sense of time. They said, when she asked, that she'd been in three weeks. It felt more like three months, or three years, or a lifetime. Who cared? Life had no meaning any more.

Penny and Vanessa were both constant visitors, and on rare occasions Bruce too. Once Flo came with a handful of tulips and a big smile and a plea to hurry and get better. But there was no rush. She might as well spend the rest of her life here, for what good it was to her.

She had nightmares. Time and time again she relived the horror of falling, of spinning and sliding, of rolling and bumping. In her dreams the downward slide never stopped.

And always before her eyes was a vision of her own face, evil, hollow-eyed, chanting over and over again, 'I wish you were dead. I wish you were dead.' And then the blank mask of Lucas, white and still—and all the time they never stopped spinning.

Only once was the dream different. Only once did she manage to put in a word for her own defence. The car came to a shuddering stop. Alina could not believe it. She threw herself at him. 'Lucas darling, I didn't mean it! Oh, Lucas, I love you—I always have, I always will. Oh, please, Lucas, forgive me, don't die, don't die!'

She woke with her own words echoing in her ears. It was daytime, which was strange; she did not normally sleep in the day. She tried never to sleep. She tried to avoid these shattering, recurring nightmares.

Vanessa sat by the bed, smiling softly, looking at her sympathetically.

'I'm sorry,' said Alina. 'How long have you been here?'

'A few minutes, no more. You were dreaming.'

'A nightmare,' admitted Alina. 'I keep having them. I keep reliving the crash. It's agony!'

Vanessa picked up a face-cloth and wiped her beaded brow. 'I know, the doctor told me. They'll fade in time.' She put the flannel away and her back was to Alina when she said, 'Do you really love Lucas?'

So she had been talking out loud! She nodded sadly.

'I'm sorry, I didn't want you to know. I suppose it doesn't matter now, though.'

'Do you want to talk about it?'

'If you don't mind?' It would be a relief. 'You are remarkable, Vanessa. I don't know anyone else who would still be friends with me after what I've done.'

The redhaired girl took her hands firmly. 'Alina, you're pretty exceptional yourself.'

Alina shook her head. 'I don't think so. When you first came to Wythenhall Manor I saw how it was with you and Lucas and I wanted to scratch your eyes out. But you were so good to me, especially when I had 'flu, that I couldn't do anything but like you. Perhaps it was as well you didn't know I loved Lucas then, or you'd probably have made me suffer.'

Vanessa smiled and shook her head. 'I doubt it. So it was more than a crush you had on him all those years ago?'

'We were going to get married, but something happened, and I never saw him again, not until he turned up and——'

'Took over Wythenhall Manor? No wonder you resented him. But it must have been a pretty powerful love to survive all that happened?'

Alina sighed and grimaced. 'Powerful maybe, painful, heartbreaking, stupid—call it what you like. It didn't get me anywhere. And now——' Tears welled and she could not go on.

Vanessa made a strangled sound in her throat and gathered Alina into her arms. 'Oh, my poor Alina. My poor, poor Alina! Why should you suffer?' She held her close for a further minute and Alina felt Vanessa's tears mingling with her own, and then she had gone, racing from the room as if in a panic.

Alina felt confused. Vanessa's reaction was not what she had expected. It was difficult to believe that she was sorry for her, Alina, when it should be the other way round. And why had she rushed away? Perhaps she would discover the answer the next time she came.

But it was Penny who turned up that evening, with the surprising news that Vanessa had gone to London.

'Why?' asked Alina.

Penny shrugged. 'She didn't say.' But she did not quite look at Alina as she said it. Vanessa must have been more upset over Alina's part in Lucas's accident than she admitted, and now her confession that she loved him had been the last straw. She was unable to keep up a brave front any longer.

Alina felt distraught. 'I told Vanessa I loved Lucas,' she said quietly, so calmly that she frightened herself. 'That's why she's gone. Now she hates me even more than she did before.'

'Vanessa never hated you,' said Penny soothingly.

'She must have. It was my fault she lost Lucas. Penny, I can't put up with much more. Penny, help me, *please*!'

CHAPTER ELEVEN

THREE months later Alina left hospital, reasonably fit after the agony of learning to walk all over again. Emotionally, though, she was scarred for life.

Penny had sold her house in London and bought a cottage in the village. 'I've decided I like the country life,' she declared stoutly. 'When you're well enough to run your shop I shall open one of my own. Crafts perhaps—or a picture gallery.'

Days resumed their normal pattern. The conference centre continued to do well. A new secretary had replaced Vanessa, but Alina saw little of her. She was a quiet mousey girl who did her job well but kept herself very much to herself.

Somewhere along the line she had missed the summer. The red-gold of autumn appeared and she took long walks through the grounds, strengthening her weakened leg muscles, scuffling her feet in the leaves, thinking, always thinking.

And then the first snows of winter fell and she rarely went out. Bruce had formed some sort of friendship with the mousey secretary and she saw little of him, but Penny was a constant visitor.

They watched television, or played records, or experimented in the kitchen. They discussed anything and everything—except Lucas!

One evening the television was on, but they were not particularly watching it. Alina and Penny were discussing a knitting pattern. Penny's eldest daughter had become pregnant, so out had come the white wool and the needles and Penny was full of the joy of becoming a grandmother.

Out of the corner of her eye Alina saw a figure on the screen. She stopped talking, her mouth fell open, and cold shivers raced up and down her spine. There was no mistaking that deep sexy voice, that gleaming pale hair.

'Penny?' She thought she was going to faint. 'Penny?'

Penny looked guilty as hell.

'Tell me I'm seeing things! Lucas is dead. It's not him, is it?' Her voice was rising. And she was cold, freezing cold, and rooted to her chair, her eyes glued to the screen.

'Lucas Delgado is, of course, quite an expert on this subject and——' The voice was stifled as Penny abruptly got up and switched off the set.

She sat down next to Alina, her face grave. 'Alina, my dear, I think it's about time you learned the truth. If Lucas slates me for it, so be it. We've all kept quiet long enough.'

What was she talking about? Was she crazy? Or was it she, Alina, who was going out of her mind? Lucas couldn't be alive. He couldn't! She had seen him lying there, blood all over his face, as still as a corpse!

'Penny, what's it all about?' Her voice was a strangled whisper.

And Penny's face looked as anguished as her own. 'Lucas didn't want you to know.'

So he was alive! All this heartache, all this torment, for nothing! 'But why, Penny? Why?'

Penny heaved a sigh. 'Apparently you told him— you—wished he was dead. So he decided, when he heard that you thought he was dead, to—to let you go on thinking it. We all thought he was mad—but no one goes against Lucas's wishes, as you know.'

'And he's alive, and he's in London?' She felt like a robot, waiting to be switched on before she could move. 'He must hate me very much.'

Tears gathered and welled slowly over. Robots don't cry, she thought, and began to laugh, and then realised that if she was not careful she could become hysterical.

Penny found some brandy and poured her a glass. 'Drink it,' she ordered. 'I know you don't touch the stuff, but this is medicinal.'

Alina closed her eyes and drank. She choked and coughed and spluttered as the liquid burned her throat, but it warmed and soothed and after a minute she felt better. But it did not relieve the agony.

She had known when Lucas returned that he was a changed man. Hard and dangerous, sometimes cruel, but never had she believed that he could be so ruthlessly inhuman as to do this.

'Lucas doesn't hate you,' said Penny, sitting down again. 'He loves you.'

'Rubbish!' The woman was being ridiculous, trying to soften the blow. 'He wouldn't have made me suffer if he did. Penny, you've no idea what I've gone through!'

'I can guess. My heart's gone out to you over and over again.'

Alina nodded. 'But your loyalty lay with Lucas? He must be some man to get people to do that for him.'

'He must be some man to love you after what you did to him.'

'*If* he loves me,' scoffed Alina. 'But how was I to know the car would go off the road? He goaded me, a girl can only take so much.' Surely she could understand that? Everyone knew what a perfect pig Lucas was to her at times.

'I'm not on about that,' said Penny. 'I mean when

you gave him his marching orders. You really hurt
him then, Alina. I know you were only sixteen, and
you probably didn't know what you were doing to
him, but even so——'

'Penny!' Alina shook her. Something was dreadfully
wrong. 'What are you talking about? Who's told you
that?'

The woman looked surprised by Alina's sudden
attack. 'Lucas, of course. I think he felt he owed me an
explanation. Are you denying it?'

'I damn well am!' she exploded. 'And forgive me for
swearing, but if that's the tale he's been spreading I
really do wish I'd finished him off. Hell, Penny, I
wouldn't do a thing like that. I loved him then, I love
him now. I always have and I always will.'

'Then suppose you tell me your version?' suggested
Penny softly.

'My version?' Alina was incensed. 'The truth, you
mean. And the truth was that *he* left me. I had my
bags packed, everything, and he never turned up. I
think I cried for a week non-stop. How the hell can he
say I sent him away? Answer me that, Penny. How can
he?'

Penny was looking thoroughly confused. 'I think
that somewhere between you you've got your lines
mixed.'

Mixed, twisted, tangled, irrevocably knotted. Oh,
what a mess! Alina shook her head, totally bewildered.
'Penny, can I have another brandy?'

'Getting drunk won't solve your problems,' Penny
said, but nevertheless poured her a small one. 'I think
the best thing you two can do is get together and sort
it all out. It's something you should have done years
ago. I wish I'd known before.'

This time Alina sipped her drink, one slow sip after
another, making up her mind that there was only one

solution. 'I'm not going to see Lucas, Penny. Not now, not ever. He has Vanessa. Once she discovered I loved him she couldn't wait to run back to London and grab him—just in case I learned he was still alive and got to him first.'

Penny shook her head sadly. 'It wasn't like that at all. Vanessa doesn't love Lucas—I've found that out. She was in love with the idea of being in love. They're very very good friends, that's all. The only way she's indispensable to him is so far as his work is concerned.'

'Then why did she go to him?' Did the woman think her a complete idiot?

'To try and make him see sense. She was devastated when you confessed. She had no idea. She thought you'd had nothing more than an infatuation all those years ago.'

'Lucas told her that.' The admission was bitter.

'Lucas told me as well.'

'I still don't want to speak to him,' said Alina, finishing the brandy and quite liking the warm feeling inside her. 'It's best this way. I mean, if Vanessa's told him I love him and he still doesn't want to come back then that's it. It's all over—finished. And Penny, promise you won't go behind my back and try to engineer a meeting? It won't work—I won't let it.'

Penny smiled and nodded. 'If that's what you want. But I think you're a fool. If I were you I'd take one of those sleeping pills you had from the hospital, together with the brandy it should knock you out good and proper. You'll feel different tomorrow.'

Would she? Fate was dealing one cruel blow after another. She was beginning to expect them. Perhaps in time she would become immune. Perhaps even enjoy them?

She did not take the pill. Her nightmares still

occurred with alarming frequency and she preferred to lie awake rather than inflict that punishment on herself.

But as the long hours stretched interminably she began to wish she had. Which was worse, reliving the car crash, or the knowledge that Lucas did not want to see her again? Penny kept her word, but a couple of weeks later Bruce had a message from Sally and raced back to London. As there was no one else to take his place at short notice Lucas came to do the job himself.

Alina kept carefully out of his way. Only once did she catch sight of him, but it was enough to tear her to pieces, and she knew that if they met face to face it would be fatal.

Perhaps, though, it was inevitable that they would meet. Wythenhall Manor was a huge place, but not big enough for two people living under the same roof not to come across each other at some time.

She was coming in, her day's work done. He was going out. She tried to avoid looking at him, stepping to one side so that he could pass. But he remained blocking the doorway.

Inevitably her eyes were drawn to his. He had not changed much—cheeks a little more gaunt, scars where she had scratched his face, but he was still handsome, still able to twist her heart. She felt the tight knot within her breast and without realising what she was doing placed her hand over it.

'Are you protecting yourself from me?'

The mockery in his voice released all she had bottled up these last few months. 'From you?' Her brown eyes flashed. 'Why should I do that? I know perfectly well that you don't care a damn about me. And just for the record, I don't care about you either. Will you please move and let me in?'

It was cold. Snow was forecast, north-easterly winds

blew across the courtyard. Alina wrapped her coat more closely about her, pulled her woollen hat down over her ears.

But Lucas did not move. His sheepskin jacket kept out the cold. She did not expect that he would feel it anyway. He had a thick skin, tough and impenetrable. No one or nothing could pierce it.

'I don't see the point in standing here like this.' Her voice was very firm and very quiet. Damn the man, why was he obstructing her? 'We have nothing to say to each other.'

A strange gleam entered his eyes. 'Maybe you haven't, but I have.' He gripped her elbow suddenly and painfully and pushed her inside. 'I think your flat. It's more private.'

He propelled her so quickly she had to run, tripping up the stairs, fumbling with her key, finally finding herself leaning breathlessly against the wall of her sitting room.

She refused to sit. As soon as he had said whatever it was he wanted to say he could go. But now that he had her here he seemed in no hurry. He shrugged out of his coat. Beneath it he wore a dark suit, and he took off that jacket too.

His ultra-white shirt complemented the tan still darkening his strong features. Alina felt a raw surge of desire, squashing it instantly, folding her arms and saying tightly, 'Why are we here?'

Lucas sat down, pulling a cigar out of a packet and taking a long time in lighting it. 'Isn't it obvious?'

'No, it's not,' she snapped.

'There are things that need saying, Alina. I've been talking to Penny, and she passed on a piece of information that somewhat surprised me.' His dark eyes watched her closely.

Alina shrugged. 'There are lots of things that have

surprised me, what's new about that?' But wait till she saw Penny! Just because he was here it did not mean the promise still didn't hold good.

'It appears you said that I was the one at fault. That I left you high and dry?'

His anger was being carefully contained, but even from across the room Alina could see the lines of strain about his nose and mouth. 'It's true—you did.'

'Dammit, Alina, why make up lies like that?' He pushed himself up so violently that it startled her. 'I know what happened. Your mother distinctly said that——'

'My mother?' Alina was across the room in a flash. 'This has nothing to do with my mother. It was your decision, your choice. What are you talking about?'

She stood in front of him, her head tilted, angry flashing eyes almost filling her face. There were mere inches between them, but at this precise moment her only feelings were disgust. How dared he try to lay the blame on her mother!

'Your message, the one your mother passed on to me—that's what I'm talking about.' His hands fell on her shoulders, big and heavy, fingers digging into her soft flesh, thumbs holding up her chin so that she was compelled to look at him.

Alina felt faint, and somewhere in the depths of her mind unease was beginning to stir. 'I didn't give my mother a message.' She sounded troubled. 'You're lying, Lucas. Why?' But all of a sudden she was not sure.

'I never lie, not about things that are important— you know that.'

'You lied when you said you were marrying Vanessa.' Heavens, why bring her into it now when there were far more important issues at stake?

He smiled grimly. 'If you think back carefully I

never gave you a definite answer. I let you assume it. It served my purpose.'

'And I suppose it serves your purpose now to lay the blame on my mother—just because she's no longer here to defend herself?' Oh, heavens, his thumbs were caressing her neck. Why was he doing that? Alina swallowed a sudden constricting lump in her throat and tried unsuccessfully to free herself.

'I wish your mother was there,' he said. 'It looks to me as though she's caused one hell of a lot of unnecessary anguish, both on your part and mine.'

It was too much to take. But she knew who she wanted to believe. Suddenly her head swam and her legs buckled. As if from a distance she heard Lucas call her name and just before she lost consciousness felt herself swung up into a pair of strong arms.

It could have been no more than a few seconds before her eyes fluttered open again. She was lying on her bed. Lucas was bending over her, a very worried expression on his face, fumbling with the buttons at her neck.

'You look ghastly,' he said. 'Do you often faint like this?'

Alina managed a weak smile. 'Only when I discover I've misjudged the man I love.'

He looked at her as though she was delirious, but a beautiful, incredulous smile began to curve his lips. 'Say that again, Alina. I don't think I heard you correctly.'

She felt his weight on the bed beside her, a warm hand caressing her cheek. 'I'm still not altogether fit from the accident, I don't know what I'm saying.' She wished she knew what had possessed her to make such a declaration. She wished she could retract it.

His thumb stroked her mouth, tenderly pulling down her lower lip so that he could kiss its soft moistness. 'Maybe you need a little practice, Alina, my love. It's been almost nine years now since you last spoke those words.'

And she wouldn't have said it today if he hadn't got her at a disadvantage. 'Did my mother really say that I didn't want to see you again?'

He nodded, lips grim for a second before they resumed their exploration of her face.

Alina began to cry, silently, effortlessly. Large tears rolling down her cheeks. She felt unutterably sad. Her mother had done what she thought was best, she mustn't hold it against her.

Lucas cursed. 'Hell's bells, Alina, don't cry!' He wiped away her tears with a corner of the sheet, and she thought for a moment that he was going to cry too.

'I feel sorry for my mother,' she said quietly. 'She wanted so much and she had so little.'

'She parted us,' said Lucas gruffly. 'How can you be so forgiving?'

Alina's smile was sweet. 'Because, Lucas, my darling, our love has stood the test of time. It should be all the better for it.' She lowered her lashes demurely. 'At least, I'm assuming you still love me? You haven't told me so.'

'Do I have to?' he groaned. 'Oh, God, Alina, I've been a man demented! I've lived nine years of hell. Only my work saved me from going out of my mind.' Unable to control himself any longer, he pulled her savagely against the hard warmth of him, ravaging her mouth with hungry insistent kisses.

Alina clung, responding with a passion she had known was there but which even so frightened her with its intensity. The urgent thudding of his heart beat against her breast, at long last admitting his love.

Finally, when Alina's head had spun until she thought she was going to pass out again, he stopped.

Dark, glittering eyes looked into hers. 'You must have hated me very much when you thought I'd deserted you?'

She stroked back the strong fair hair from his proud brow, holding his infinitely precious head between her hands. 'I was confused. I was hurt. But I never, never hated you, Lucas. I might have told myself I did, but I know now that I never stopped loving you. You're part of me, Lucas. Without you I'm no good.'

He looked strangely humble. 'Nor me without you. It was as though all these years only half of me has been living.'

She giggled. 'If only half of you can make a million, think what two halves can do!'

'I might have known!' He tried to look angry. 'You're only marrying me for my money.'

Alina wriggled away. 'I've not yet heard you ask me to marry you, Lucas Delgado. And in any case, I'm not so sure that my answer will be yes.'

With surprising swiftness he pulled her on top of him. 'You've no choice. My mind is made up.'

His long body was hard and warm beneath her and she moved ecstatically. 'What a bossy man you've become!'

'Just because I know what's good for you?' They rubbed noses and smiled into each other's eyes, and then their hungry passion again took over. Alina could have let him go on kissing her for ever and she knew that it was with reluctance that he eventually put her away from him, rolling off the bed, combing his hair. 'Hell, I could do with a drink.'

'There's whisky in the other room,' she said. 'And I'll have a brandy.'

He looked surprised.

'For medicinal purposes only,' she informed him. 'I

don't want to faint again. I might miss one of your kisses.'

He poured their drinks and then stood with his back to the fireplace. 'What puzzles me, Alina, is why you lied, why you told me that you'd fallen out of love with me. I imagined that you woke up in a cold sweat on your sixteenth birthday thinking, "God, what am I letting myself in for? I can't marry a man like him. I don't love him." Why didn't you tell me the truth as soon as I came back?'

'How could I? Heavens, Lucas, I had my pride. So far as I was concerned you'd walked out on me. When you turned up without one word of explanation, not even an apology, I wanted to hate you. I told myself I did.'

'But you couldn't make a very good job of convincing yourself? I'm glad, Alina. I've been a swine since I returned, and I know it, but you made me so mad. I thought you should be apologising to me.'

He finished his Scotch and poured another. 'I knew you were still physically attracted, and for a while I tried to get you to admit that you still loved me. Then I was going to drop you like a red-hot brick!'

'I wondered why you kept trying to kiss me,' she laughed. 'You're not only a swine, Lucas, but a devious one as well. I'm not so sure that I want to marry a drunken, devious swine.'

'You'll do as you're told,' he said fiercely, putting down his glass and moving menacingly towards her.

She walked into his arms willingly. 'You don't frighten me any more,' and she looked at him, smiling gently, touching his scars and knowing they would be a constant reminder. 'Once, before you became a man, I could wrap you round my little finger. Now you're the boss, and I'm your willing servant.'

'God, no!' He crushed her to him. 'We're equals,

Alina. We're a partnership. Whatever decisions we make we make together.'

'Like handling the conference centre?' A dimple showed in her cheek.

He groaned. 'Alina, please, don't make me feel even worse. I must have been insane. It was a ridiculous contract. Oh, my love, how I must have hurt you!'

'Not only that,' she said, determined to make him suffer, 'you almost made me close down my shop.'

'Only because I wanted you to be solely dependent on me.' He held her close, his head buried in her hair, and she felt him trembling.

'But let's get one thing straight. I'd already decided to open a chain of shops in the Cotswolds before I became involved here. I must admit, though, that I did price everything ridiculously low—often for less than I'd paid. And I stopped you buying at the sales. I'm sorry. I did try to make up, though. All my shops had instructions to send customers to you.'

Her eyes widened. 'It wasn't Flo?'

'Lord, no!' he laughed. 'Maybe she tried, she's a good woman, but you don't really think she'd have that much influence?'

'I must admit I thought it surprising. Tell me, Lucas, why did you answer my advert?'

He tilted her chin, looking at her. 'How can you escape the pull of a magnet? Eight years I'd struggled against it. There comes a time when a man can fight no more. I'll tell you something else, though. I was coming back anyway, one day. When your mother told me I wasn't good enough for you——'

Alina winced but let him go on.

'I made up my mind to show her whether I was good enough or not. That's what kept me going all those years, Alina. I was making my fortune, yes, but with one goal in mind. I was going to come back and buy Wythenhall Manor. I was going to make your mother an offer she couldn't afford to turn down.'

She closed her eyes. 'I feel awful,' she whispered. 'I had no idea. She consoled me when you left. She was so good to me.'

'And with what justification,' exclaimed Lucas bitterly, 'when she'd ruined both our lives? I know what I'd like to call her, but I won't. Perhaps it's as well things happened as they did.'

For a moment he looked so grim that it frightened Alina. She looked at him plaintively. 'Lucas?'

Then he relaxed and smiled and held her close. 'First thing in the morning I'll see about the marriage licence. Then, as soon as Bruce returns, we'll go away. How does a cruise round the Greek islands sound?'

'You took Vanessa round the Greek islands,' she accused. 'I thought you loved her. She loved you—she told me so.'

He smiled ruefully. 'We had a brief affair, but that's all it was. We ended up, surprisingly, being good friends.' He kissed her hair. 'Mmm, you smell nice. I must admit I did use her to make you jealous, and naturally she preened herself over it. But I shall always be in her debt for telling me that you loved me. She's quite a girl, is Vanessa. She told me off good and proper.'

'But you still didn't come back?'

'I didn't believe her. I *wouldn't* believe her. When I woke up in hospital and discovered all I'd suffered was a few cuts and bruises I went absolutely berserk. Did they tell you that? I tried all ways to kill myself. I think they thought they'd got a maniac on their hands. I really believed that you wanted me dead. Then when I realised that no way was I going to die, it seemed the best solution all round to let you think I had.'

'Lucas, what can I say?' Her eyes were full of pain. 'I reckon you don't feel any worse than I do, letting you lie in that hospital bed, never visiting you, adding insult to injury by pretending to be dead. Please, Alina, tell me you forgive me. Tell me you love me. Tell me over and over again. Tell me for the rest of your life.'

She smiled. 'That will be easy.'

He began to kiss her uncontrollably, then roughly put her from him. 'Hell, this is no good. I'm going to give Bruce a ring, see when he's coming back—I can't wait to take you away from here and get you on my own.'

He dialled the number and while waiting for an answer said, 'Alina, you and Bruce. Did he—was there——?'

She shook her head. 'He was a friend, when I needed one, that's all. But while we're on the subject, what did you mean when you said he was going to destroy me?'

He shrugged. 'The way I saw it, a man who's been divorced is certainly not going to get involved again. I thought he'd use you. In fact there were times when I hoped he would. I wanted to see him toss you aside like you had me.'

And then Bruce was on the line. Lucas listened and smiled and agreed, then turned to Alina. 'He's coming back—tomorrow. He's bringing Sally with him. Would you believe it—they're getting married again! They're going to make a new start here.'

Alina was pleased, he deserved a second chance. 'So it's new starts for all of us, darling?'

He grinned and pulled her into his arms. 'Not for us, we're simply going to carry on where we left off nearly nine years ago. We're going to forget what happened in between.'

She lifted her lips to his. 'Forget what, Lucas? I don't know what you're talking about.'

Harlequin Plus

A WORD ABOUT THE AUTHOR

Margaret Mayo was born a twin, the younger of the pair by an hour. Her twin brother was her constant companion during her childhood in Wednesbury, a small town in the industrial Midlands of England.

When she married, Margaret moved to another town not far from her birthplace and, after several years, began her own family. During all this time, she had no inkling that she would ever become a writer. In fact, she was a secretary in an engineering firm when the writing bug first bit. She began to scribble a short story in some spare moments, and though it was never published, it led to her second work, which was published, and eventually to the thirty or more novels that now bear her name.

She lives with her family in a large house in the English countryside, where she writes full time and enjoys the constant company of Sam, the family's cocker spaniel. Margaret remarks, "He lies at my side all day making sympathetic noises when I complain that nothing is going right, sleeping soundly when the words steadily flow and my electric typewriter hums."

4 FREE

Harlequin Romances